BATTLE WHALE

THERE SHE BLOWS...YOU TO PIECES!

ALAN SPENCER

BATTLE WHALE

ISBN: 978-1-925342-27-7

PART ONE: FIRST STRIKE

LAUNCH DAY

Green World spared no expense building the ultimate weapon. When it comes to environmentalists, we're the cream of the crop, and we've got a mega-sized blue whale to prove it! Can you picture six-hundred short tons of beauty lunging at you with rockets thrusting, machine gun turrets blazing, and heat-seeking missiles set to kill? I sure can, because it's right in front of me. That'll teach the evil ones who perpetrate evil against nature. You can't talk people down from their wicked ways. You can't assign legislature to protect our beautiful animal creatures. We can't trust things will just get better on their own. Doing the right thing isn't as easy as promoting morality.

So where does that leave the people who really do care?

The answer?

Battle Whale.

Nobody can hold us back from our aspirations. Green World is an organized, well-funded, highly educated, super environmentalist group. We've pooled our resources over many years to get the job done. We can't wait to see our whale at work.

It's almost time.

I can't stop shaking.

I'm so excited for this moment.

You see that oil drilling rig on the Pacific Ocean? It looks like the real thing, but guess what? It's a decoy. We're inside of it, conducting our work. Battle Whale will shake the world to its core. No more animals will be harmed, *ever*, after our plan takes effect. Humans will fear the animals. It's the way it has to be. We'll finally achieve that delicate balance of power. Whether our wonderful animals reside in the oceans, the jungles, the cities, society will leave nature as God intended—the fuck alone! The world will hear our voice, even if we have to blow their guts out to do so. Sacrifices on both sides of the coin, animal and human, will have to be made, but it's for the greater good of the future.

Green World is the future.

The anticipation is really starting to set in. I'm pacing and my heart's pumping like crazy. Good thing I've been taking medication for my ticker or I might just keel over.

Battle Whale is scheduled to attack in two minutes and counting. Go ahead and kiss the illegal whaling industry goodbye. That's just the humble beginning of the plan.

The first strike.

You want to throw harpoon grenades at our ocean's beautiful creatures? You want to steal the ocean's beauty for its blubber? Then we've got something *real* special for you. Stupid bastards are going to pay with their blood.

Two minutes and counting.

Yes, yes, yes, yes.

That gives me barely enough time to really reflect on our accomplishments before the big moment. This project has been in the running for six years. Private investors have spent billions to make this happen. These are the people who truly champion the cause. They know buying organic, shopping at Whole Foods, and recycling isn't enough to really change things.

The International Whaling Commission claims to have curbed illegal whaling, but the whale populations keep decreasing. You can't always trust what you're being told. Facts and figures can be altered to benefit those in power.

Battle Whale will show them what's right and plow through their deceptions.

Currently, I'm standing here among my fellows in celebration. We've surrounded the giant aquarium where our Battle Whale awaits deployment. Corks are popping. Wine flutes are overflowing with bubbly. Fists are pumping. Jovial conversations are spreading. Kisses and hugs and fond memories are being shared. This is it!

For me, the celebration is the whale itself. I'm a marine biologist. I can't help but watch that special whale float in its enclosure and marvel. The blue whale is a beautiful creature on its own terms. The whale is massive grayish-white beast. Most of its bulk is in the front of its body, while at the back, the body gets sleeker towards the tail. I'm just a speck up against its enormity. I'm nothing.

Our Battle Whale is almost unrecognizable in its current form. Steel covers over seventy percent of its body. Circuitry, wires, satellite uplinks (this baby is plugged in!), armor, hardcore thrusting engines, and fold-out wings, our whale has been crafted with scientific, aeronautic, avian, naval, wireless, and defensive precision.

Under that armor are reserves of supplies. Rocket-guided missiles by the hundreds. Bullets big enough to load giant cannons; bullets large enough to turn humans into vapor. Liquid napalm to burn entire cities. Nitrous oxide to fuel many high-speed travels. Sulfuric acid to melt enemy vessels. Mortar shells. Giant harpoons with explosive tips. Concentrated batteries the size of cars. This whale is equipped for a variety wide-scale attacks.

Everybody has had their hands in this endeavor. I tended to the whale's basic needs like feeding, habitat upkeep, and general welfare. Others were heavier cogs in the machine. Ballistics experts. Mechanical and structural engineers. Fiber-optics specialists. NASA scientists. Blacksmiths, metallurgists, computer programmers, weapons specialists, the list goes on and on. Hundreds of brave volunteers joined up with Green World to make this happen.

The world won't stop harming animals and that's the bottom line. It's up to somebody to stand up for what's right. What's more symbolic than an actual animal standing up for its own rights?

If this test run goes off without a hitch, we won't stop at whales. Every species, every phylum, kingdom, and genus of animal will rise up and stand up to humanity until peace is the end result. We will equip every animal to protect itself. Finally, this will be a fair right.

Thirty seconds and counting.

Okay, I'll indulge in some sparkling champagne. Why not? We're overworked, exhausted, and very determined to see this project into fruition.

Twenty seconds and counting.

All eyes are on the digital clock beside the giant whale tank. Many are counting down out loud. I keep watching without saying a word. I'm amazed at what we've accomplished. This event will propel us into a new future.

Red and green lights flash along Battle Whale's steel armor. Engines from head to tail are raging with pistons and power. The water in the tank is spilling over the top in crazy tidal waves. The whale's beady black eyes now glow an ultraviolet red.

Five seconds.

Four seconds.

Three seconds.

Two seconds.

Engaged!

The bottom of the tank opens. Battle Whale drops down from the tall-standing oil rig platform and splashes into the ocean. Nitrous is burning and the Battle Whale is a streak of motion underwater, traveling at one hundred and twenty miles an hour and increasing speed.

The whale's cries rage across the ocean, the pitch reaching over 80 Hz frequency and still rising. The whale's piercing calls draw fear and awe into the other ocean dwellers. From everybody on the rig, this inspires reverence.

Now the satellite uplink station hidden in the United States has control over Battle Whale via remote signal. It's up to them to complete the job successfully.

The rest of the project is out of our hands.

Everybody's celebrating the successful launch. I notice Rhonda Geason, my blonde assistant, is giving me the "come hither" look. Sex is gleaming in her eyes, and I for one, am ready for a little loving between the sheets. I might be old, but my dick sure still works. I bring Rhonda in for a kiss, and—

BLAST 'EM!

The battle whale had cleared two hundred miles from the drop sight before the military descended upon Green World's ocean base like a merciless fury. Helicopters unloaded armed officers onto the base. They repelled from ropes, invading the tall-standing steel pillar made to look like an oil rig.

Four-star General Sam Hudson laughed from his chopper view as his boys reduced the dangerous hippies into shredded cabbage with their guns. Hudson could smoke cigars and watch his team in action all day and never get bored. The Green World terrorists, as Hudson labeled them, were nothing against his forces.

Blood, bodies, and smoking guns.
All in a day's work.
And God love it.

Ten minutes later, Hudson received the go ahead to touch down on the base and conduct his investigation. The general was very curious about what Green World was perpetrating out in the middle of the Pacific Ocean.

General Hudson was stepping over still-bleeding corpses as he scouted the long steel platform for information. There was nothing of interest here, except for plenty of dead assholes. Inside the base was another story altogether. The smell of heavy smoke weighed heavily on the air. Raging fires were being put out by officers all across the three levels.

"Bastards were trying to destroy evidence," the general said to a representative of the FBI, a tight-assed, to-the-point suit named Chris Blevins. "Once they saw us coming, they tried to cover up everything. This was a well-oiled machine. I still want to know the point of this tower."

Blevins surveyed the area. He didn't respond. Blevins pointed at the giant steel tank across from where they stood. "Anything inside that?"

The general followed Blevins up the stairs to the next level. They stared down into the tank. There was no bottom. They could see down into the ocean.

"Whatever was in here, it's gone now," the general said. "Any idea what it was?"

Blevins stooped down, blew on the edge of a clipboard that was still burning, and put out the fire. He pointed at the drawing of a giant whale.

"It's a blue whale, General."

"What the heck were they doing here out in the middle of the ocean with a whale?"

Before General Hudson could attempt a guess, officers were reporting about what they found scattered throughout the rig. The consensus: everything informative was burned black.

Blevins sighed. "Looks like there's no answers here. We're too late. Our Intel was on the money, but late, as usual. Looks like I'll have to go back to the bureau and come up with a new plan."

General Hudson wasn't sure what to make of the FBI agent. He was a skinny prick with a rod shoved up his ass and he worked as if the general wasn't even there. Screw it, Hudson thought, him and his boys had done their job. The next move was up to some up other schmuck with a higher pay grade and more monkeys on their back.

Blevins stayed behind. The general re-boarded his chopper. A new chopper had just landed. The transport was full of FBI men dressed in suits and another set were wearing Hazmat uniforms. The general knew they were identifying the corpses of Green World. There was a lot of red tape to cut and Hudson was grateful he wasn't the one lugging around the heavy scissors.

My job's done here.

Every drop of blood has been spilled that needed to be.

Enough said.

When the chopper was posed above the platform, Hudson could see Blevins instructing his staff with a new verve he hadn't seen in the man up to this point.

The general couldn't help but ask himself that insane question again, *Just what in the hell was Green World doing with a whale?*

OCEAN ASSAULT

Battle Whale had them in its sights. Using its long-range viewfinder sensors, it locked onto a fleet of Nordic whaling ships scattered about in a semi-circle formation. The ships themselves were at work collecting the afternoon's take. Cannons and harpoon grenades had made short work of a collection of whales. The men were working on lugging the whale corpses up into their vessels. They didn't see the threat coming, until it was too late.

The whale's eyes burned a brighter shade of red. Rising up from the ice-cold Antarctic waters and bursting up like a cannon ball, steel wings unfolded at both sides of its body and held strong. Rocket thrusters under those wings unleashed giant balls of flames and propelled the mass over the whaling fleet.

Whalers cried out in terror as the beast's shadow eclipsed the now ants up against this berg of power. Battle Whale was a machine of sleek grace, flying high enough to drop bombs from its wing turrets. Nail bombs, incendiary bombs, and grapeshot-inspired explosions reduced ship and crew into smoking smithereens. Explosions tore the fleets asunder, changing the ocean into a fiery spectacle of death.

The whalers who abandoned ship before the bombs dropped suffered the worst fate. Steel nozzles extended from the whale's lower torso and unleashed a shower of liquid napalm. Shrieks split the cold gray skies as skin sizzled, boiled, and evaporated from bones. The victims' skeletons floated like charcoal-black buoys.

Before Battle Whale plunged back into the ocean, those on the mainland could hear the whale's high-pitched songs of pleasure rip through the barren cold skies.

Toji Maru understood deadlines were deadlines. Japan's whaling industry was a highly lucrative and highly illegal trade. There were strict regulations on how many whales could be killed in a specific period of time. Toji could tell you what to do with those regulations, and how far they could be lodged up one's rectal cavity. Money was the name of the game, and Toji played it to maximum profit.

Factory ships were loading up dead whales onto their boats via conveyor belts beneath their ships. Toji's team was efficient. The key was speed. If they could mine the fruits of the sea and pay off the right people to look the other way, Toji and his company were in for a big pay day. Whale meat, blubber, cosmetics, it was all cash. Fin whales. Sperm whales. Hunchback whales. Mink whales. Sei whales.

Toji pictured fat stacks of cash piling and piling.

As long as there was gold in the sea, he would be there to mine it.

Toji shouted orders into his radio at the factory ships to bust more ass. Today, his team wasn't as effective as normal. People were people and sometimes you couldn't make them work hard. Toji was about to chew into another ship captain because of his lackadaisical progress when the ship to his right was lifted up and seemingly thrown into the air. Wooden beams shattered, engines burst, and the ship was turned into fodder mid-air. What touched down among the wreckage was something he couldn't describe.

A flash of steel. Green and red lights. Demon eyes. Cannons blazing. Five thousand bullets were unloaded into Toji's fleet of thirteen whaling ships instantaneously. He literally saw some of his best men dismembered by impossibly huge bullets. They were like grenades rendering arms, legs, heads, and guts into chewed up mess.

Toji's ship was the last vessel remaining intact. The enormous hunk of steel was posed in front of his ship. The longer he stared, Toji realized the mass was actually the head of a blue whale. It wore a strange steel crown. Its red eyes seemed to seer into Toji and reach into the very core of his soul. A sharp whinnying cry ripped across the ocean with such power, Toji thought it was from supersonic speakers. Both of Toji's ear drums burst. He landed on his knees, crying out in pain. From between the whale's eyes a steel device unfolded. It was a long and thin nozzle of a cannon. The cannon's tip pressed against Toji's chest. The last thing he heard was the whale's taunting, insane song before a trigger was engaged.

Toji erupted into pink mist. Those who would later comb the ocean for remains of the crew would find Toji's hands held together, as if begging for mercy.

Battle Whale emptied another five hundred rounds of machine gun fire into the ship, targeting the individuals on board, and then channeling the bursts into the engines. Toji's ship was burning bright when the whale made its successful retreat.

Andreas Askar was the captain of the Nordic ship fifty nautical miles from the first whale attack. He received the report of the attack, and Andreas couldn't believe it. Andreas absorbed the facts, and he still couldn't accept them. One thing was for certain. He was going to pull up the anchor and get the hell back to the mainland.

The anchor wasn't moving.

Why wasn't the anchor moving?

After arguing with his co-pilots, they came to a stark-raving mad conclusion: there was no anchor. So what the hell was keeping them in place, Andreas demanded of his staff. Those words were instantly downgraded to waterlogged-garbled cries of terror. The vessel was pulled underwater, as if someone was tugging on a string connected to the bottom of the ship. Freezing cold water rushed into the cabin. Andreas clutched onto the wheel to brace his body as the ship was jarred by forces coming in at them from all angles.

The shock of everything was elevated by what was right in front of him. Moving specks of demon red eyes. The high-pitched noises of a wretched song sung in the name of death. Part-whale, part-machine, he was facing off with the monster who had connected the ship's anchor to its own body.

Andreas stared in increasing fascination of the mega-whale until a series of sensor-guided missiles obliterated his ship, and everything, including his own body, was turned into fodder for the bottom dwellers of the ocean to feed upon.

Five cargo ships were delivering the slaughtered bodies of Northern Bottlenose whales from the Faroe Islands. Mining the Denmark territory for whale and dolphin meat was easy fat cash. American, John Wright, was the captain of the main vessel. The ocean was a thing of beauty he thought, and a thing of money. John loved the smell of the ocean, and he loved the smell of fresh blood. That meant their time here at sea was successful.

John walked the open area where whalers were cutting the heads off the whales and spraying them down with water. This was the very beginning of the packaging process. They would later pack them up in ice and deliver them back to the mainland. John's men crafted their blades with precision. He was about to give his men words of encouragement, and that bonuses were in their future if they put out that extra bit of effort.

Before he got the first word out, something that clanged like a tin can landed between his hips. It had bounced, bounced, bounced, and then stopped between his feet. The can was the size of a diesel truck's gas tank. John was surprised it hadn't punched a hole through his ship. When the giant can turned, he noticed a stamp on the green can.

Green World.

Oh God no.

Where the hell are those bastards?

John was moments from calling his ships and telling them to watch out for protestors when a giant rushing wall of water obscured the horizon. He couldn't make sense of it until it was over. It was like the ocean was blasting a geyser of water into the air. Steel reflected the sun, as did the whale skin he was used to seeing bleed out on his boat. The gigantic whale flung its steel-covered tail so hard at the ships that, one-by-one, it turned them all into pieces.

John backed up and tripped over the giant can. Triggered by a flashing sensor light, thick green smoke hissed from the can. Pain soon arrived, and it was only going to increase in intensity up until his final moments of agony.

The green spread like fog, reaching out to everybody on the ship in under twenty seconds. Reactions were a waste of time. Calling out for help was equally a waste. John had breathed in plenty of the noxious fumes before covering up his mouth. Five seconds later, his throat melted. His lungs fizzled into carbonated blood. John coughed up his tongue and esophagus, and what landed in his hands cut right through them to splatter against the ship.

Before he could garble out a plea of terror, his intestines leaked out of his ass in a clotted stream, and his steaming brains oozed out of his socket holes. When the local police spotted John's ship drifting aimlessly and boarded the vessel, all they found were human puddles of gore.

Battle Whale utilized its cloaking device and remained invisible on all naval radar. There was one more task to complete before the mission was complete. Arriving in the Gulf of Mexico, Battle Whale's collection of rocket-guided missiles was armed. Each rocket was charted for a specific course. Rockets blasted from its back, shooting up out of the water, and traveling across the sky to destroy over fifty factories involved in the whaling industry. Once its rockets were used up, Battle Whale lowered down into the ocean, went into hibernation mode, and awaited its next set of orders.

CELEBRATION

Nora Keever couldn't contain herself. She cheered, then threw her hands around her fellow Green World members, in the main control room. There were only twelve of them, including Nora's daughter, Sasha. Everybody watched the control panels, the screens, as they monitored Battle Whale's health status, location, and armament supplies. The mission worked without a hitch. The members killed out in the ocean would be proud. Nora Keever was determined to carry on the legacy of the message. Green World would be heard. Nobody could ignore their plight anymore. Not with Battle Whale fully functional.

After celebrating, Nora searched for her daughter. She asked around and found that Sasha had left the room moments ago. The sixteen year old had an attitude problem. It was more than hormones and being a teenager. Why couldn't she hammer home the importance of their work to her daughter? Sasha questioned everything. Nora knew she had to be patient with the girl. Her daughter's youth got in the way of understanding why blood had to be shed to get their point across to the world.

One day, Sasha would bleed green, Nora vowed.

Nora exited the main control room. She entered a narrow hallway with a concrete floor and walls carved out of a cave. They were located in St. Joseph, Missouri, three stories deep underground. This was the main satellite where they could plug in orders to the Battle Whale. This is where everything was made possible.

Nora next searched the mess hall, a tiny square cut out of rock with canned goods lining a series of shelves, and two long fold-up tables and chairs. There was Sasha, the blonde-haired lovely who would break a lot of hearts. She had matured early into a young woman and the boys were always lusting after her. Sasha wasn't the type to put up with whistles and stares. She talked like a seasoned sailor when necessary and didn't mind punching someone if they got out of line. Nora was proud of her daughter, but it when it came to the cause, Sasha's convictions were seriously lacking.

Sasha had her head down against the table. Her shoulders were heaving, because the girl was crying. Sasha's tears didn't draw sympathy. It drove Nora to anger.

"Get up out of that chair and quit crying, Sasha. You're ruining our moment. We've worked so hard to make this happen, and you're being a brat! Buck up and raise your head. This is our time to do good work."

Sasha shot up out of her chair. Her face was cherry with anger. "*I'm* being a brat? Sorry I don't like murdering people. I saw those feeds on all of those screens back in the control room. Those people on that one ship, they, they, they melted! You guys clapped. You were smiling like a bunch of idiots. It's sickening. I don't want any part of this. Why can't I leave? You made me come here. You pulled me out of school and forced me away from my friends. You forced me away from everything that made me happy, and I've been hiding in this damn cave for a whole year. I hate it in this cave. I'm going to lose it. I've got cave fever. There's no one to talk to, except you crazy people. I don't think what you're doing here is right. There's other ways to get your message across besides slaughtering people, there's got to be--"

Nora raised her open hand, and slapped Sasha hard across the face.

Sasha's nose was bleeding from the blow.

Sasha wept. "You've been a bitch ever since you left Dad. I think you're crazy, Mother! Stay away from me!"

Nora tried to run after her daughter, but she restrained herself. If she went after her now, what else would she do to her daughter in frustration? No, it was best she let the girl go. Nora knew there was no way to escape the cave. Each access required a password, and Sasha didn't have that information, so her ungrateful daughter could have her fit. Sasha would have to learn the messages behind Green World and take them to heart, and if that didn't happen soon now that the mission was a success, Nora wasn't sure about Sasha's future here in the cave.

SASHA KEEVER

Sasha's body trembled. She was so angry, sweat burned like acid against her skin. Her mother, her step-father, and Green World, all the crazy idiots, they could all go drop off the face of the earth. Green World was a cult who would one day drink the poison Kool-Aid, and Sasha hoped that one day was today. What kind of parents pointed a gun at their daughter and forced her to enter a cave and hide out for a year? They were essentially terrorists. If it wasn't for Xavier, Sasha wouldn't be scared to fight back.

Xavier, Sasha's step-father, was a murderer and a slick sociopath. The man had changed her mother. The members of Green World were brainwashed, and Xavier kept them that way. The fearless leader, Xavier, threatened to kill her mother if Sasha didn't go along with Green World's plan. Nora didn't know this. If Sasha told on him, Xavier promised to kill them both. What else could she do in this escalating predicament but go along with what he demanded? She felt so helpless.

Sasha ran to her room, what was merely a hole cut out of rock with a blanket hanging over the entry as a door. She had to try something and call out for help. There was only one man who cared about her, who really loved her, and would do anything to save her.

Her real father.

Mack Keever.

The problem, her cell phone didn't get a signal. She kept trying to call him every night before going to bed. This was her only retaliation against the group.

When she tried to text him this time, Sasha did get a signal

Sasha's fingers typed fast and nervously. *Dad, I really do love you. It was Xavier. He made me lie. I never hated you. I'm in danger. Mother, she's lost it. They're behind the whale attack. They're planning so much more. We're at that point—*

Sasha couldn't finish. Her wrist was seized. It felt like her hand was being crushed.

"What are you doing, Sa-sha!"

The cell phone was wrenched from her grip. A snarling Xavier bashed it against the rock wall. "I thought we got rid of your phone. I told you no contact with anyone. You jeopardize so much, you stupid girl. You do this on purpose!"

Xavier, the bald-headed juggernaut at two-hundred and fifty pounds, was a human bull. He seized Sasha's neck with both hands. "I'd kill you right now, if it weren't for your mother. I'd bury you and forget you. Stupid little bitch. You do this on today, of all days, when everything's going so well. I never considered you my daughter, and I never will. Your real father can have you. You're not my blood. My blood wouldn't do something like this!"

Sasha almost lost her bladder. Xavier's rage made his face the color of a choked-off artery. His animal face warned Sasha that he'd killed and would continue to kill for his beliefs. She didn't realize she was being strangled until the man released his hold. Sasha coughed and nearly puked. Xavier didn't give her a chance to fully recover. He twisted her arm behind her back and dragged her out of her room. He pushed her forward with little effort. Xavier was cursing and muttering unintelligible things. He sounded like a possessed man having a seizure.

Her step-father would kill her.

That much Sasha knew to be true.

And Xavier was the type to convince her mother that her being dead would be the greatest thing since the building of Battle Whale.

Xavier used his free hand to open the door to the supplies room. There was toilet paper, laundry detergent, and sanitary supplies lining the shelves on the walls. Sasha was thrown against the floor. The back of her head hit a mop bucket. Sasha curled up into a ball and prayed the man didn't stomp her to death.

Instead, the door slammed closed. The door was locked from the other side. Sasha could hear Xavier and her mother talking under their breaths from the other side.

"She has to die," Xavier whispered. "She texted on her phone. She's jeopardizing all of our work. I know she's your daughter, and I tried to love her too, but it's the only way. We've already lost a lot of people on the team. There's not many left who know how to operate Battle Whale. We're it, for now, until the organization can regroup. We can't afford even the smallest screw up."

Sasha didn't recognize her mother's voice.

It was dead of emotion.

Evil.

"I agree. I've tried everything to win her over. I swore to myself I wouldn't give up on her, but I think you're right."

Xavier seemed pleased.

"Then we'll talk about the most humane way of taking care of the problem."

Those words chilled Sasha. She wasn't going to die without a fight. There was one hope tucked in the back of her mind. Somehow, some way, her father received that text, and he would find a way to save her from these murdering, overzealous environmentalists.

Oh, how she prayed.

PART TWO: DARK TIMES

NIGHT VISIT

Mack Keever slept hard on his couch. Someone standing outside his house would be able to vaguely hear the two-hundred and sixty pound boar of a man snore. Mack had split a bottle of bourbon with his best friend, Jack (Jacky Boy) Williamson tonight, and they played acoustic guitars all night. It's what two people who ran a guitar shop in Ralston, Missouri, on a Saturday night did to entertain themselves. They would drink until their fingers couldn't grip the fret boards anymore.

Mack slept deep because of the alcohol, though his mind spun with worries.

His daughter, Sasha, hadn't talked to him in two years. What she texted him earlier today was perplexing:

Dad, I really do love you. It was Xavier. He made me lie. I never hated you. I'm in danger. Mother, she's lost it. They're behind the whale attack. We're at that point—

Maybe Sasha had spent the night at one of her girlfriend's, and they were drinking, and Sasha decided to drink and text her father. That made the most logical sense. There was anger and ridiculousness in that text. Jack told Mack one time his daughter had sent him a series of texts that were meant for her boyfriend.

Dirty stuff, Mack. You could've read it in one of those Penthouse *magazine letters. I could've hunted down her boyfriend and smashed a guitar over his head. I figured my girl had enough punishments once she figured it was me she sent those texts to. Girl still doesn't look at me the same.*

Mack texted Sasha back, but he didn't receive a response.

Drink and dial, Mack determined. Sasha was probably as drunk as him tonight.

Mack hit a little bong, a lot of bourbon, and it being three in the morning, Mack and Jack were passed out and wandering deep into dreamland.

It startled them like a bolt of lightning striking their heads what happened next. The front door was kicked in. Every window access in the house was smashed to pieces. Before Mack could lift his head up off the pillow, he was grabbed by three men covered in black with scary night vision eye gear. The machine guns kept him quiet, even when one of those who'd entered picked up his Gibson guitar and stomped it into three pieces. Other intruders were destroying his massive LP collection. Another stomped his bong into bits.

Without a word, they were lifted off the couch, handcuffed hands behind their backs, forced out the front door, and escorted into the back of what looked like a paddy wagon.

Mack couldn't see his friend in the dark.

He sat on the steel bench, and tried to sort out what had just happened.

Jack asked, "Were they the police? They didn't read us our rights."

"I don't think the police smash into your house like that," Mack said. "Assholes. That one had no reason to smash my guitar. He did it just to be a dick. And my LP's, man. Fuck."

"It's because we were smoking weed. They have new machines that can detect when you toke up. They're cracking down."

"A team of people wouldn't do all that over a couple of spent roaches and a bong. It'll be okay, Jack. You know what I always say? It's not a problem until it's a problem. This has to be a misunderstanding."

"One hell of a misunderstanding. You pay your taxes, Mack?"

"This isn't about taxes, but yes, I do."

"You're not selling drugs, are you?"

"No! You're being ridiculous. I haven't sold a dime bag since eighth grade. My dad caught me and he smoked it all up, then spanked my ass raw. I still feel it when I sit down sometimes."

"Aren't you worried?" Jack was breathing hard. "What if they're going to kill us?"

"Two washed up musicians, yeah right. Of all the threats against America, Mack and Jack rank pretty low."

"They think we're terrorists. Oh no, man. They'll lock us up without a reason, and they won't let us out. They can do that now, ever since 9/11."

"It's not a problem until it's a problem. We'll be okay. Do yourself a favor and stop talking. You're going to give yourself a coronary. Truth be told, I'm a bit nervous, but I know this is someone's fuck up. Someone's going to buy me a new Gibson, and they're going to fix my front door and all my windows. I bet all kinds of bugs are getting into my house right now, damn it."

"How can you be worried about bugs in your house right now? We're being taken by strangers with machine guns off into the night. You only read about this on TV."

"You mean you only *hear* about this on TV," Mack corrected. "Stop talking, and just breathe. Imagine yourself at the Zebra Club. We've just played a flawless gig, and you've got two women, and let's be realistic, they're kind of slutty, and a bit rough around the edges, and they want to join us backstage and blow us."

Jack didn't respond.

Mack couldn't hear him breathing.

"Jack? *Jack.* Are you okay? Answer me, man. Jack!"

The vehicle stopped. Before Mack could see if his friend was okay, a blaring white light blinded him. Somebody forced a hood over his head. Mack could barely breathe because he was shouting so loud for Jack. Three men had to carry him sideways out of the vehicle because Mack was thrashing and crying out, and he would keep crying as he was forced to go somewhere unknown against his will.

INTERROGATION

"Take that, fat boy! You're going to spill everything. You're my bitch. Take it like you're a bad guy, because that's what you are. The bad men who do bad things to good people deserve to have their faces rearranged. That's you, Mack Keever. I'm putting you down as bad guy number one. You're no better than a terrorist. I don't know what kind of a fucked up life you've had. I'm sure your daddy touched you where he shouldn't have, while your mommy watched and laughed. Who knows the extent of your kinky lifestyle? I'm sure if you painted a picture, you'd need every color.

"Being fucked up in the head doesn't give you the right to take it out on honest-to-God good people. I'm going to take great pleasure in stomping in that face of yours. I know torture techniques. I practically wrote the book. I even drew the pretty little pictures in it. Your busted mug will be on the front page of a revised edition at the rate we're going."

Sucker punch. Gut punch. Jaw punch. Kidney sock. Front kick to the solar plexus. Elbow driver to the chest. Two finger jab beneath the armpits.

Mack didn't know what hit him, but he knew one thing, and that was how he wished for this bastard to stop.

Mack stayed on the ground, playing it smart. He'd had more than enough of a beating. He bled from his nose and both sides of his mouth. Mack clutched his belly with both hands. Everywhere hurt. He shared the room with a human beating machine. Mack wanted out of this trap, but he knew there was no way out, except to endure more pain, so he stayed right where he was, safe on the ground.

The room had four walls, a light bulb at the ceiling, and a smooth concrete floor. The ceiling was exposed. Mack imagined they were in the basement of an unfinished house. This was a great place for a person to be killed, buried, and forgotten without a single shred of evidence left behind. Mack was surprised, and relieved, because there wasn't plastic lining the walls.

The man who beat the hell out of Mack came in close and unfolded a chair. This stranger was a tough-looking man with a flat top haircut, ripped biceps, bulging chest, and a black suit jacket. This man had to be in his mid-forties. The man placed the chair under the ceiling light and pointed a stern finger at it.

"Get up, fuck face. I have some questions for you, Mack, or do my fists ask you instead? Don't play with me, Keever. It chaps my ass when people play dumb with me. I've rearranged your guts and your face long enough for you to know nobody's going to come out of the woodwork and fight for your rights. You answer to me. You're all mine, pal. I can paint this room with your blood. The United States of America have given me the divine right and privilege to extract information from you in any way I deem necessary. And when someone gives me, Agent Freddy Stones, this privilege, I damn well use it. So sit down and answer my questions. Either way, we're in for an enlightening evening, Mr. Keever."

Mack had to scrape himself up off of the floor. Fresh blood leaked from his nostrils. He spat it away when the red crossed his lips. Mack's voice didn't sound like his own. He imagined someone removing his voice box and replacing it with an angrier, more determined version of himself. Considering he was a bourbon-drinking, guitar playing, pot smoking, laid back fuck-off in general, the ruggedness of his voice was quite alarming to himself.

Mack wouldn't be the same after tonight, or ever again.

"What happened to my friend?"

"You mean Jack Williamson?"

"Yeah, asshole. What happened to Jack?"

"Heart failure happened. Tough break. Sorry."

Jack had been his best friend since they were in elementary school. They survived life together in every way: money problems, women problems, band problems, best friend problems, and this Agent Stones fuck-head announced Jack's death like it meant absolutely nothing to anybody in the world.

It meant something to him.

Mack's hands were cuffed in front of him, but he bunched his fists together, launched up from the chair, and slammed both of his hands into Stones' belly. The agent let out a shocked "Oaf!" Mack raced up the stairs, stepping over the fallen agent, but there were two men on top of the staircase aiming machine guns at him.

He stopped where he stood.

"I got this," Stones said, slightly out of breath. "He got one on me. That's my fault. I let my guard down. It won't happen again. Now sit down, Mack, or you get shot down."

Mack stared at the men poised on the stairs. The look in their faces was as cold and calculating as Stones' menacing expression. Mack knew they would turn him inside out with machine gunfire and enjoy a coffee break afterwards.

Agent Stones calmly said, "Sit down, Mr. Keever. This is a matter of national security."

"National security? What? You're mad. You've clearly got the wrong guy. Now my friend's dead because you put him through hell tonight. I'm going to—"

Stones grabbed him by the neck, forced him down into the chair, and jammed a Ruger pistol under his chin. "You're going to sit, listen, answer my questions, and leave out the rest. If you were smart, you'd want to hear what I have to say. It involves your daughter."

"Sasha?"

"Yes, Sasha."

Mack thought back to the text he received earlier tonight. Maybe there was something to all of this. What that could be exactly would make for an interesting story to tell someone after this terrible night was long over and done.

"Then I'm listening, dickhead," Mack said. "You people are going to pay for Jack. I'll save that for later."

Stones didn't talk about Jack, so he moved on. "Okay, I'm looking at you, Mr. Keever, and I don't see who I'm supposed to be seeing. You own Guitar Mania, you teach kids guitar lessons, you tend to a business, and you play shitty music on your off-time. You reek of weed and bourbon. You're nothing special to me."

"Then why the fuck am I here?"

"Tell me about your ex-wife?"

"Who, Nora? Why bring *her* up?"

"Tell me about when you last heard from her."

"I don't hear from her. We divorced years ago. Around the time we divorced, I owned my guitar shop, and Nora decided to go back to school and earn a degree in marine biology. She met that Xavier guy in one of her classes, and he brainwashed her. Xavier's one of those, you know, Green World guys. He swept Nora up into his ideology. Those Green World people are crazy. Like extremists. I want nothing to do with them."

"Keep going, Mr. Keever."

The agent's face was pure concentration. As long as the man wasn't throwing anymore bullet-fast punches, Mack would keep talking.

"Xavier's a psychotic. He reminds of Charles Manson. He can manipulate people to his will. The bastard repels me. He even stole my daughter from me. Sasha didn't want anything to do with me because of him. Sasha told me to my face that Xavier was a better father than me. She really broke my heart.

"Look, man, I understand I probably spent too much time pursuing my blues music, but I was there for my wife and daughter. I paid the bills, I was a good father to Sasha, and I did my very best to keep things fun and romantic with my wife. I can look at it objectively and say I was a good dad.

"It's Xavier. He brainwashed those two. I tried to win them back, but I couldn't. Next thing I know, I'm sending my child support checks to some foreign P.O. Box, and Sasha and Nora are traveling from place to place across the country fighting battles on the behalf of Green World. I feel like my ex-wife cast me out of my daughter's life. Xavier won the battle. I didn't stand a chance against the guy. I guess I'm not slimy slick enough."

"If that's the case," Stone asked, drawing in closer to Mack, "then why did Sasha text you during the whale attacks?"

Mack spluttered, "The *whaaaaaat*?"

"You know what I said."

"Do I? Whale attacks? Man, you're kidding me! Maybe you beat me up too hard earlier. My heads ringing. I have no idea what you mean. This isn't the best time to be pulling me. And what are you anyway? FBI? CIA? PETA? I should ask you for some identification."

"I'm Agent Stones. CIA. I'm not showing you my identification. I don't have anything to prove to you. It's you, Mr. Keever, that needs to answer some questions, and you better wipe that grin off of your face before I smear it with blood."

When Agent Stones cracked his knuckles, and Mack remembered what those fists could do, he immediately returned to being serious.

"So yeah, okay, whale attacks. Can you please tell me what you're referring to, Agent Stones? I haven't been in contact with my family for a very long time. Sasha won't see me. That text puzzles me now that you point some things out. Do you have my cell phone? I want to read the text again. I was pretty drunk earlier. When you kicked the shit out of me, it sobered me up. Thank you for that. You were as refreshing as a hot cup of black coffee."

Agent Stones had the text memorized.

He dictated it verbatim.

"*Dad, I really do love you. It was Xavier. He made me lie. I never hated you. I'm in danger. Mother, she's lost it. They're behind the whale attack. We're at that point--*"

Now that Mack was clear-headed, it sounded like Sasha was in trouble. Mack instantly made the connection.

"What does Nora and Xavier have to do with these terrorist attacks?"

"Whale attacks," Stones corrected. "Green World has really outdone themselves this go around. They've planted bombs at manufacturing plants, freed animals at animal testing facilities, and murdered those who supported legislature that supported the so-called harming of the environment in the past. But this, *this*, trumps everything.

"Xavier's one of the topmost leaders of the movement, and Nora's at his stead. Judging by Sasha's text, she's been forced into supporting the cause. She was reaching out to you for help. This is what we know, and where you come in, Mr. Keever. There was a base out in the middle of the Pacific Ocean where Green World gathered some of the world's topmost scientists, biologists, and military personnel to create the ultimate weapon. Green World decided to turn a blue whale into a killing machine.

"This is no joke. I see you about to laugh again, Mr. Keever. I'm going to give you five across the mouth if you even snigger. Whaling vessels from Norway, Iceland, and Japan have been decimated. Same as dozens of whaling factories. Rocket-guided missiles have turned them into toothpaste. Now we can't locate the whale. This baby's off-the-radar. This is cutting edge technology. Dangerous technology. The world's in danger. Everybody.

"Here's the deal, Mr. Keever. Your daughter is clearly in danger too. If I'm guessing correctly, whatever signal controls this whale, Xavier and Nora are behind it. Your daughter is probably sitting ringside and terrified for her life. You can save her. Please, if there's anything in that text that can help us locate her, that'd be most helpful."

"Why can't you track her down by Sasha's cell phone?"

"Can't," Stones sighed. "There's more to this attack than a whale loaded up with missiles. Many of our frequencies are jammed up. We can't trace calls. The military can barely maintain contract with each other. I'm separated from my superiors. Green World is up to more than we realized. Phone lines, communication lines, everything is jammed up."

"What is Green World really up to?"

"Global domination, maybe, or universal protection all of animals, or…"

"Or, what?"

"Or Green Peace wants to destroy every human in the world, except for the loyalist of Green World's members. Start from scratch, you know, protect the environment, with a clean slate, after all the blood they've spilled has been mopped up and the bodies buried, of course."

"Jesus," Mack gasped. "You're serious."

"So I want you to think about that text, and if there's any clue as to where they could be hiding out, or anything at all, please."

Mack couldn't believe the woman he used to love was essentially a murderer and a world-wide terrorist. And he still couldn't picture a whale covered in weapons. That was simply ridiculous. While Mack was thinking this, Agent Stones opened a laptop computer and showed Mack feeds of the whale in action, as it blasted whaling vessels into exploding pyres.

"This is for real," Mack said. "No, the text doesn't ring any alarm bells."

"Keep repeating the text in your mind, Mr. Keever. There might be something in those words, something cryptic. I'm grasping at straws here. I'm stuck here with my agents with nothing to do. We're to lay low until new orders arrive, or I get vital information. Something big is going down, and I can't let it happen."

Mack was staring at the computer's screen, then the Internet feed went down.

"No signal, Agent."

"What?" Agent Stones' face tensed. "The Internet's down, the phone lines are down. Nothing's working."

"What are we going to do now?"

The agent's face was no longer the confident, bad ass. He was scared. "We wait, Mr. Keever, and hope to hear from somebody soon."

Mack couldn't shake the unsettled feeling from his body. Trouble was ahead, he kept thinking, and the agent was right. Trouble was all the world would be seeing very soon.

WE HAVE TO KILL HER

Xavier held Nora in his arms. They were standing outside the control room. The very room that controlled every function of their prized whale killing machine. Ten elite members of Green World were tending to Battle Whale's status inside. Weapons were at eighty-nine percent. Battery power was eighty-two percent. Health: one-hundred percent. The whale was invisible, off any radar detection, practically off the grid, and hiding in the Gulf of Mexico.

Things were going perfectly.

Now, Xavier could focus on his step-daughter. Sasha jeopardized everything. Nora was good and subservient. He liked women he could mold and re-mold. Nora was the perfect woman. Anything he wanted her to be, Nora would transform into it at a whim. But Sasha, she didn't support the cause. Not truly. Sasha was independent, anti-everything Green World, and like any teenager, out-of-control.

Sasha would have to die. He couldn't have anymore close calls. If their position was given up, that would be the end of Battle Whale. So many had died, sacrificed, and toiled hard to give the world back to nature. A little brat wasn't going to spoil Green World's overall plan.

Xavier stroked Nora's long brown hair streaked in gray. Nora had a comely face and eyes that reminded him of a dog. Eyes that said "love me" and "don't hurt me" in the same gaze. Xavier was the master, and Nora was the subservient bitch. Some women needed a man to take control, and Xavier was happy to be the one to do it.

"I'll kill her for you," Xavier said, soothing Nora. "I'll make it easy. No pain. I have a pill. It'll make Sasha fall asleep. Then her heart will stop. No pain. It'll be instant."

"It won't hurt?" Nora started to cry. "You promise me it won't hurt."

I'll stick her like a fucking pig. I'll rip her heart out. I'm going to take her into the other room, lock her up, strip her naked, and give her something I've always wanted to give that pretty little bitch. Nobody has to know. My pretty peach. The mother's nectar is sweet, but the offspring is always the sweetest.

Xavier held Nora closer to him. "I promise. Sasha will feel no pain. You understand why we're doing this, don't you? Everything we've worked for can either be successful or ruined in the coming days. Sasha could do something that might kill us all. Our efforts would be for nothing, if that happened."

"Yes, I know." Nora could barely talk; she was so grief-stricken. "I thought Sasha would come along. That she would grow to believe what Green World is trying to accomplish."

"Sometimes what we want for the people we love isn't what they want for themselves. Do you want to be there when it happens? When she dies, I mean?"

Nora sucked in a breath and suddenly came alive. "No, I can't do it! I can't kill my own daughter. You keep clutching that knife at your belt. You don't have a pill. You're a liar! How dare you ask me to harm Sasha? I thought you said that because you were mad at her. I never thought you'd actually do it. You son-of-a-bitch! I've made so many sacrifices for you. I've practically followed you into hell. I've done everything you wanted me to do, and you can't give me one thing, this one thing. My own daughter!"

Nora was beating her fists against his chest, slapping him, raking her claws into his neck, and Xavier didn't feel any of it. This was the moment he knew Nora was just like her daughter. Nora was once malleable clay, and now, the bitch was dried up and useless to him.

It was time to throw her away.

Xavier seized Nora's neck, and in one violent jerk, he snapped the woman's neck. Nora collapsed with a mixed expression of horror and anger on her features. Xavier dragged her into his private room and draped the corpse across his bed. He would deal with her body later. For now, he had to make sure the Battle Whale was fully functional for the next step in the plan.

In a couple of hours, he would be carving up some soft female flesh. Sasha's sweet girl flesh. He would watch muscle and skin slide off of his knife. Xavier would carve her up into something unrecognizable. He would relish every inch of her body from top-to-bottom. Then bury her so deep into the ground.

Nobody challenged Green World and lived.

THE THREAT TO OUR GREAT NATION

Xavier composed himself, wiped the sweat from his bald head, and changed into a green army uniform. He strapped on an AK-47 for visual effect. Beside the control room was another room where he would sit at a desk while two of his men filmed him. His message would be broadcasted to the entire world. He would hijack every TV channel. Their signal was that powerful. Their signal also had another special ability. Xavier could already visualize the blood flowing in the streets of America and the rest of the world.

Gibbons and Percy were arranging their equipment to film Xavier. Gibbons gave Xavier a countdown to five, and once he counted down to one, Xavier took a breath, and addressed the world.

"Hello, my name is Xavier, and I have a very important message to deliver on the behalf of Green World. We are behind the attacks against the whaling industry." Xavier knew Gibbons and Percy were showing footage of Battle Whale destroying boats during his speech. "Our Battle Whale is equipped with many weapons. The Battle

Whale is also equipped to deliver a special message to the world."

On the screen, a long list of companies, products, causes, and those involved with poaching animals, and using them for testing products, were showed on the screen.

"I want these companies and groups responsible for the harming of our wonderful creatures that God bestowed to the world disassembled, and if need be, executed with extreme prejudice. Our whaling industry attack was a simple demonstration. We can, and will, back up our threats.

"Our whale can deliver a special signal that will attack your TV stations, your radio waves, and your wireless signals. All animals will rise up and take back the world, which is rightfully theirs, if you can't do what's right on your own. No matter what you do, Green World wins. If you want to be a part of a better world, then I suggest you do as I say. You have twelve hours, or we'll give the world back to the creatures that originally inhabited it. Looks like I got you by the balls, America. It's up to you if, and when, I let go of them."

That ended the message.

Xavier set his watch to twelve hours.

Now, they would wait.

POWER SURGE

Xavier, immediately after delivering his message, entered the control room. Walls of screens, control panels, and launch systems occupied the room, alongside four of Green Peace's best operatives. Xavier inquired about Battle Whale's systems.

"Fully operational, sir," Dodge Claymore said, the senior-most member of Green World. "Battle Whale's ready for the next phase. Whenever you want us to turn on that signal, all systems are go. Hundreds of types of animals, even some insects, will pick up on our signal. They'll deliver the message. *Kill all humans*."

"Very good," Xavier said. "Hey, what's with all the static on those screens?"

"There's been a few lightning storms in the area. The lightning has been striking really close to our satellite dish. Let's hope we don't get struck, or else there could be some serious technical difficulties. The weather wasn't supposed to be—"

A wicked crack of thunder later, a bolt of lightning struck their main satellite tower above ground. Dodge didn't have a chance to finish his sentence. Showers of sparks blasted from every console. Dodge was thrown back from his chair with a charred black face and skin bubbling like hot pizza cheese. The three others at their desks were cooked to a crisp right down to the bone. Xavier didn't realize he'd been thrown back against the wall. He'd struck the back of his head against the rock wall. He was blinking stars out of his eyes.

Was he hallucinating, or was the control panel now working on its own? Buttons were being pressed, systems were being engaged, and what was that God-awful sound?

Eeeeeeeeeeeeeeaaaaaaaaaaaaaaaaaaaa!

The song of a whale.

The high-piercing, aquatic song, penetrated his brain. Xavier clutched both sides of his head and cried out in agony. Messages were beating down into his brain. The whale's cries were like commands.

Obey me. Fight for me.

Do as I say.

I command you.

Kill all humans.

Blood dribbled from his nose, flowed from his tear ducts, and burbled from his ear drums. He was being consumed by the message.

Xavier spoke like an automaton. "I must protect the signal. Kill…all…humans."

Eeeeeeeeeeeeeeaaaaaaaaaaaaaaaaaaaa!

Eeeeeeeeeeeeeeaaaaaaaaaaaaaaaaaaaa!

Eeeeeeeeeeeeeeaaaaaaaaaaaaaaaaaaaa!

Xavier was intoxicated by the song; he was no longer repelled by it. He craved the sound. Many things were spoken in those messages. Save the world from destructive humans. Protect nature, and its friends, at all costs.

Animals unite.

Battle Whale's song couldn't be ignored.

Xavier claimed the helm of the control panel. He would ensure Battle Whale's commands were obeyed.

Eeeeeeeeeeeeeeaaaaaaaaaaaaaaaaaaa!

Eeeeeeeeeeeeeeaaaaaaaaaaaaaaaaaaa!

Eeeeeeeeeeeeeeaaaaaaaaaaaaaaaaaaa!

Battle Whale had spoken.

Every human must die.

No more waiting.

SONG OF BATTLE WHALE

The satellite tower in St. Joseph, Missouri, was crackling with bluish electricity. This super-charged the original signal, warping it into something evil and potent across the United States. Battle Whale, hunkered down in the Gulf of Mexico, near the Texas shoreline, received these messages. The radio wave receivers and wireless capabilities built into its steel exterior communicated the messages through the wail's song.

Eeeeeeeeeeeeeaaaaaaaaaaaaaaaaaaa!
Eeeeeeeeeeeeeaaaaaaaaaaaaaaaaaaa!
Eeeeeeeeeeeeeaaaaaaaaaaaaaaaaaaa!
KILL ALL HUMANS!
KILL ALL HUMANS!
KILL ALL HUMANS!

The message attached itself to every television, radio, and Internet feed. Everywhere, the people of the United States, and the world, could only hear the whale's deadly song.

Battle Whale's engine revved up, blowing a storm of bubbles up to the ocean's surface. Moments from unleashing its next attack, the

Battle Whale would make good on what Green World started.

Nature would retake the world, and reclaim it as its own.

PART THREE: ANIMAL RAGE

GULF OF MEXICO

Aaron Long enjoyed peaceful protests. It was a great way to spread a positive message of peace and of respecting Mother Earth. And above all else, it was a surefire way to get some pussy. He wasn't the most handsome guy in the world, nor was he good at slinging the English at the ladies, but whenever he joined up with the hippies and conservationists at Texas University, he always had female company. He was surrounded by over two thousand peaceful protesters, most of whom were women. He faced the Gulf of Mexico on a long pier and waved protest signs. The sun was beginning to set. The backdrop of orange would soon turn to a purple within the hour.

Aaron's sign read: RESPECT THE WHALE! It was the best he could muster, but he could do worse. He read the variety of messages on other signs:

GO WITH WHALE, YOU CAN'T FAIL
BATTLE WHALE FOR PRESIDENT
NATURE IS MAKING A SPLASH
FISH HAVE FEELINGS TOO
RESPECT THE EARTH OR DIE!

CONDEMN THE WHALING INDUSTRY
THE WHALE HAS EVENED THE ODDS
NATURE AND HUMANS FINALLY ARE EQUALS
NO MORE CRUELTY TO ALL ANIMALS, GO VEGAN!
GREEN WORLD FOREVER!

Some of the college kids were dressed up in whale costumes and clutching toy machine guns, mimicking battle whale. Others were playing acoustic songs, namely about the greatness of the majestic whale. News crews were filming the event. After Green World's message to the United States went global, everybody was buzzed about the coming hours and what could happen next.

Aaron was suddenly concerned by what appeared in the ocean. Rising up from the dark water, the blunt head of blue whale, crowned by steel, peeked its head over the surface. Everybody cheered.

"We are with you, WHALE FRIEND!"

"Peace by with you, BATTLE WHALE!"

"Whales Rule!"

"We promise we will never hurt you!"

"Nature has spoken, and humanity has listened."

"No more harming any living creature."

"Battle Whale, WE LOVE YOU!"

The excitement demurred into something terrible in less than ten seconds when the noises screeched from the whale: *Eeeeeeeeeeeeeeaaaaaaaaaaaaaaaaaaaa!*

Aaron cupped his ears. The sounds only increased in decibels. Aaron could see the whale's eyes burn a brighter shade of demon red. Aaron's body was seized by the force and impact of the sound. He felt the throb, the bass, and the projection, rock his body. The vibrations delivered tremors into the wooden pier. He thought the pier could collapse any moment when the sounds of splitting wood became so intense.

Eeeeeeeeeeeeeeaaaaaaaaaaaaaaaaaaaa!
Eeeeeeeeeeeeeeaaaaaaaaaaaaaaaaaaaa!
Eeeeeeeeeeeeeeaaaaaaaaaaaaaaaaaaaa!

The vibrations attacking the pier weren't from the whale's call. Up from the sea, crawling up the legs of the pier, were hundreds upon hundreds of gray crabs with demonic red eyes flashing evil. Aaron watched people become swallowed up from head to toe with pincers clacking, raking, delving, and cutting up flesh. Blood showered down between the cracks of the pier and reddened the waters. Aaron literally watched Liza Woods, the girl he wanted to bang for the longest time, be carried away in eighty different pieces by scattering crabs.

Clack-clack-clack-clack-clack-clack-clack-clack.

Screams pierced the air, human flesh tore like weak fabric, and everybody on the pier was disembodied and plopped down in the sea, reduced to future fish food. Aaron tried to run. He slipped on wet, strung out guts, and popped dozens of eyeballs under his Birkenstock's before Aaron took a header off the edge of the pier.

Before he could swim out somewhere, anywhere, to escape, a new rumble in the sea promised him he had done nothing but stepped that much closer to certain death. Ten yards ahead of him, he was spun upside down by a great wave of power. Something massive surfaced. Engines spit out their hot thrust as the once-cherished Battle Whale rose up from the sea. Aaron could only float in position as twin cannons erupted, unleashing a wall of bullets. Aaron was reduced to eleven-hundred smoking hot pieces before Battle Whale took to the sky.

OH, THE HORROR!

Mack didn't like being in a basement in such close proximity to a CIA agent who couldn't stop chain smoking, flicking his lighter between cigarettes, and itching his hands, neck, and eyes like a withdrawal-stricken dope fiend.

"Would you stop being so fidgety?"

"Shut up, Mr. Keever. Not another word from you."

Agent Stones wasn't broken from his mental hell. He kept smoking, itching, and flicking the lighter. He threw in a few agitated sighs for good measure, between walking up and down the stairs and consorting with the other agents. Something wasn't sitting right with Mack, and whatever it was, wasn't sitting well with the agents either.

"You people aren't planning on killing me? I mean, I'm out here in the middle of nowhere, and you guys are acting...*funny*."

Mack expected another verbal backlash from the agent. What he got was a single loud laugh. "Hah! This is so much bigger than you. This is everything. The whale attacks were only the beginning. So you bet your ass I'm acting funny."

One of the agents called down to Stones. "The President's about to address the nation."

"You know what, Mr. Keever," Agent Stones said, "I can tell you're not a terrorist. It's pretty obvious. I bet your band can barely tune, never mind wire-rig a whale to blast the world to hell. You should come on up with me."

Agent Stones undid his handcuffs and helped him up out of the fold-up chair. "You promise me you won't try and run anywhere. You stay with us until you're told otherwise. If you run, I can't guarantee one of my boys won't hesitate to put a hole in the back of your head."

"I'm not going anywhere," Mack said with conviction. "You guys scare the shit out of me. You could probably make me disappear and make it look like an accident. And I don't exactly enjoy being called a terrorist. I'll stick around to clear my name. I'm okay with America. I'm not a threat. The threat's my ex-wife, that bitch, not me."

"I'm beginning to see that, buddy. Now come on up. Watch the president address the nation. The president has managed to bust through the hijacked signal long enough to broadcast. I still haven't been able to contact anyone back at the agency. Even cell phones and CB radio are fucked. All you can hear is that whale's high-pitched singing."

They walked up the stairs. The top level appeared to be an empty cabin. He recognized the woods. They were somewhere in Springfield, Missouri, maybe near Osceola. One agent was setting up a laptop computer to play the president's address. Two other agents were eying outside the windows with concerned expressions.

"Why did you pick this place?" Mack asked the agent. "It's a bit out of the way, don't you think?"

The agent messing with the computer answered that question. "We wanted you somewhere where nobody could hear you scream. The CIA had a long night of festivities planned for you, Mr. Keever. The party would begin with some friendly banter, then we'd start busting toes, pulling teeth, torching your dick with a lighter, and depending on how much you told us, or *didn't* tell us, we'd start water boarding your ass."

Mack noticed the corner of the cabin with a giant roll of plastic sheeting and a tool kit double the size of a tackle box.

Sweet God, I dodged one helluva bullet.

Nora's still making my life a living hell.

What have they done to my daughter?

Mack was suddenly worried. "Do you know anything about my daughter? Has Xavier done anything to hurt her? That man's the real danger to society."

"The entire world is in harm's way," Stones answered, "and everybody on Green World is standing safely behind the barrel of a big ass gun. We hoped whatever text Sasha sent you would help locate them. We couldn't trace it. This super signal is messing up all communication. I can't tell you if your daughter's safe or not. I'm sorry."

"*Shhh.* The president is speaking." The agents at the windows drew in close to the TV. President Ted Yearling, the pork-bellied, white-haired, greasy-palmed figurehead wasn't in his normal, confident, Bill Clinton-esque form. He was terrified, and there was no way for the man to hide it. The man's hands were trembling as they clutched the podium positioned outside of the White House.

"My fellow Americans, this broadcast won't last long, so I'll be brief. Let our military handle the situation. Nobody is to take the law into their own hands. Stay in your homes, behind locked doors, and wait for help to advise you. The threat is real, and it is powerful, and it's—"

The laptop's speakers unleashed an ear-piercing shriek: *Eeeeeeeeeeeeeeeeaaaaaaaaaa!* The reporters in the crowd cupped their ears. Many fled the scene. Up from the sky, a moving curtain of black descended upon the White House. Thousands of bats with glowing cherry eyes tore into the reporters, flensing screaming faces clean of skin, and even working together to lift people up high into the air and dropping them like sacks of concrete.

The transmission was terminated.

The laptop kept issuing that horrible whale song. Agent Stones removed his Glock and shot the computer to pieces. "Enough of that."

The three other agents were drawn to the windows. Mack heard what concerned them. There was a curious rustling coming from the woods. Mack peered into the dark woods between the trees and could see things moving closer to the cabin.

Stones took control of the situation. "Boys, get your bigger guns out. We have visitors."

Mack swallowed hard.

This was going to be one hell of a night.

RETREAT!

Secret service agents were blasting the air with their pistols as the bats descended upon the crowd of reporters and spectators at the White House. President Ted Yearling could hear the bats gnawing, chewing, and slurping blood en masse. The security team hurried on the reeling president back inside the White House. The flying beasts were angry, the way they hissed and rasped in their tiny voices. That, mixed with the whale's song, was enough to strike terror into any reasonable human being.

Bats were popping like fireworks as guns reduced them to steaming hot debris. The determined demons on wings kept coming. Agents left and right succumbed to the attacks. Necks were chewed through and severed heads were carried off like demented trophies. Others bats acted as kamikazes, their wings thrashing at the air so hard, and so fast, that they pierced through the backs of security members like bullets.

The president thought his eyes were going to pop out of his head with the things he was seeing! He caught a flock of pigeons burst through a door at the east end of the room. They pecked to death the reporters who were running up the White House lawn in retreat.

A security officer shouted, "Through here, Mr. President. Duck and stay low. We're getting you to the safe place."

"Where's my wife?" President Yearling shouted over the din of killer bats, pigeons, and that infernal whale's song. "And my daughters? You have to save them!"

The president was struck down by several heavy wet objects. Knocked down, he tried to get right back up. The secret service agents had to help him to his feet. He was soaked through in blood. The president cried in terror, seeing his wife's bloodied severed head, and his two daughters looking like they'd been run through a hungry wood chipper.

"Jesus Goddamn Uncle Sam! GET ME OUT OF HERE!"

The president did his best not to succumb to the shock of the events. He was pushed onwards through several wings of the White House until he arrived at an elevator. The last standing agent pushed him inside, then acted as a human shield as bats chomped through his every limb. The agent landed in the elevator with the president as a dripping red skeleton. The elevator closed, with one bat getting inside. The president grabbed it by both wings, ripped them off, and stomped the rest of the wretched thing into the ground with the heel of his shoe.

"Die, you savage little bastard!"

The elevator traveled three floors underground to the safety bunker. Below, there was a team of scientists, military officials, more protective service, and the vice president, who had literally pissed his pants and was currently drying himself off with a towel.

A scientist, a man almost seventy years old named Charles Gooding, grabbed the president by both arms. "For God's sake, issue the order! Send every missile, bullet, bomb, grenade, and good ol' American boy to destroy that whale. Then you must locate the signal. They've scrambled everything we've got here. We're defenseless. Kill that whale and stop that signal, or else every animal is going to turn the world into a bloody slop trough!"

President Yearling regained his breath and his gall. He wasn't going to be the like the piss-pants vice president. This required evasive action. The actions from a true leader. The world could be gone in an hour if he didn't try to combat this insane threat. Damn Green World!

"Fine, Dr. Gooding. I'll unleash everything on that goddamn whale. By the end of the night, I'll use its blubber to light my room."

Defense Secretary Duke Steinman was on top of the Executive-in-Chief's order. "You heard the president. Give that whale everything you got, and for God's sake, find the source of that signal, or all of America will become worm food!"

President Yearling watched his team in action and prayed to any and every God that somehow things would end up in America's favor.

The president removed his daughter's ear from his breast pocket, handed it to a security officer, and lit a cigar from his inner suit jacket pocket.

He certainly had serious doubts about the future.

BATTLE WHALE

Battle Whale hovered in the air above the Gulf of Mexico. The vessel knew what was coming. It could intercept any military signal ahead of time. Battle Whale engaged every weapon in retaliation. Military tanks were lined up at the edge of sea. Cannons were being set-up on the rooftops of nearby buildings. Attack jets were zooming in the sky. Aircraft carriers surrounded the shore in a half-moon formation. Submarines awaited deeper in the ocean. Military bases that dotted the nation were aiming missiles at Battle Whale.

The whale had a plan of strategy, and the mammal executed it.

Before the first whale-seeking missile was deployed, killer whales and other blue whales arrived on the scene. Missiles rocketing towards its target were intercepted by suicidal whales. Blubber was exploded, cooked, and splattered against the shoreline in gory heaps. Sea gulls drowned trying to sort out the food mess. Tank fire, B2 bomber rockets, rocket launcher blasts, they were all blocked by the sea creatures rising up from the ocean and sacrificing themselves.

The Battle Whale used the cover and instantly retaliated.

Eeeeeeeeeeeeeeeaaaaaaaaaaaa!
Eeeeeeeeeeeeeeeaaaaaaaaaaaa!
Eeeeeeeeeeeeeeeaaaaaaaaaaaa!

Five thousand rounds of .50 caliber machinegun fire tore through military tanks, igniting fuel tanks. The blasts decapitated and disembodied soldiers in mere wicked-flash seconds. Twenty incendiary missiles were unleashed from the whale's arsenal. They turned twelve city blocks into hellish burning infernos.

Eeeeeeeeeeeeeeeaaaaaaaaaaaa!

Engine thrust fueled by nitrous power drove the Battle Whale up as high as the B2 bombers and the random jet crafts circling the air. Battle Whale's cannons spread obscuring blankets of smoke. The thick mess was sucked into the engines of the jets and the air inside the jets was tainted. Super mustard gas instantly melted human flesh, turning the pilots into screaming, boiling meat pies. Jets spun out and crashed into the sea one-by-one.

Eeeeeeeeeeeeeeeaaaaaaaaaaaa!

Battle Whale locked its targets on the fleet of submarines approaching the scene.

Soooooooooooooooooooonk!
Soooooooooooooooooooonk!
Soooooooooooooooooooonk!

Deep sea missiles penetrated the waters, surged deep, and downgraded metal into crunched up aluminum cans. Long-range missiles locked onto new targets, decimating arms and munitions storage in Kansas. More missiles, more distance, dozens of military bases across the United States were engulfed in fiery death flames.

Battle Whale flew over land, over the city, as water sprayers misted the whale's body, keeping the whale alive. It unloaded every rocket, missile, and bullet from its nearly-depleted supplies.

Thoooooom!

Thoooooom!

Thoooooom!

Miles in each direction, every mode of retaliation was reduced to smoking smithereens.

Battle Whale retreated back into the Gulf.

The next phase of the plan would soon be enacted.

TRAPPED IN A CLOSET

Sasha heard her mother argue with Xavier through the door. The argument grew heated, until there was an abrupt silence. That silence applied to the entire underground compound. Nobody said a word. Nothing was happening. It made Sasha nervous. She wanted to beat down the closet door, storm out into the hallway, talk some sense into her mother, and get the hell away from Xavier forever.

But what had happened?

Why the silence?

Sasha thought on things. There was no talking to her mother. Xavier had done a wonderful job of brainwashing her mother. After Nora's mental breakdown and being diagnosed bi-polar, she returned to college to get a degree in marine biology. That's where she met Xavier on campus, and the rest was Green World history.

How many times had that sociopath threatened Sasha's life? Sasha wept, knowing how Xavier made her block out her father, Mack, out of her life.

Never again.

Xavier wasn't going to prevent her from living her life.

Sasha searched the cleaning room and spotted the mop bucket and mop. She snapped the wood handle at the end, turning it into a stake. She imagined plunging it into Xavier's vampire black heart. The bold rush of adrenaline abruptly ended when the doorknob turned from the other side. Someone was coming inside. When the door opened a crack, Sasha saw every notch of Xavier's K-bar knife. He had the blade turned downwards, as if to gut her.

"I've come to split you open, my pretty peach. First, let's have some fun!"

Sasha was repelled to the farthest wall in the room. "Stay away from me, you sadistic pervert! You've always looked at me the wrong way. I knew you were sick. I never realized what you were capable of until now."

Xavier was enjoying her display of fear. It made Sasha's body crawl in disgust, then it made her blood rush in anger. This is exactly what Xavier wanted. Sasha refused to bow down to her tormenter ever again.

Sasha lunged forward. She drove the sharp end of the mop stick into Xavier's side. Xavier cried out in shock, then pain. Sasha shoved him aside and exploded into the hall. Xavier was cursing, ranting, and wincing in pain as he worked to remove the mop stick from his torso.

She was running down the length of the facility that was reserved for living quarters. The rooms were holes cut out of the walls, with curtains draped over the fronts for doors. She stopped when she saw the leg sticking out from the curtain from one of the rooms.

It was her mother's room.

Sasha's stomach dropped.

Nora lay there staring up at the ceiling with dead glazed over eyes. Her neck was turned at an awkward angle. Sasha checked her pulse.

No pulse.

Her body was ice cold.

Sasha hugged her mother. "Mom, no! Don't leave me alone with that monster! I love you. I'm sorry for all the things I said about you. I hated him. I love you. Please, don't be dead!"

Xavier's footsteps could be heard coming nearer. He was slower moving, but his pace was getting faster by the second. His words were ripe with evil intentions.

"Your mother was sweet, Sasha, but you will be so much sweeter. I won't kill you until I've had you! And who knows? Maybe you'll like it. I'll lick you from your lips down to your toes. I'll make you moan in pleasure. You'll love every minute."

The words made every inch of her skin crawl. Sasha ran away from her mother's body to escape Xavier. If he got his lecherous hands on her, she couldn't imagine what he'd actually do to her. There wasn't anywhere else to go in the compound. Two men were stationed outside the control room. They would restrain her and give her up to Xavier.

Her options were limited.

There was a short stairwell that led into the bottommost section of the facility. There were no lights down there. Only pitch black darkness awaited her. That was her only choice, be it a bad one or not.

Sasha ran and hid into that darkness, and Xavier was coming right after her.

XAVIER IS ANGRY

Level your breathing. Stop the bleeding. Patch yourself up. That pretty little bitch isn't going anywhere. It's a dead-end down there. A bunch of random supplies storage. Plenty of places to hide, but I'll find you, my darling. Nora's death was merciful, but yours, Sasha, will last weeks. I'll string you out. I'm talking about locking you up in a basement, recording the event, and really enjoying myself. I've earned it. Green World, hell, Battle Whale, wouldn't be in existence if it weren't for my efforts. So go ahead and hide, pretty little Sasha. I'll find you, and when I get my hands on that nice body of yours, it'll be well worth it. I can't wait to taste you.

Xavier entered what served as a group shower room. He moved to a sink, removed his army fatigue shirt, and checked the wound just above his hip bone. The sharpened mop stick had entered with some depth, but it hadn't pierced any organs. He was in no danger of succumbing to his wounds. Xavier washed off the section of upturned skin that looked like an upside down pink "J" and bandaged it with the medical kit hanging on the wall.

After he put his clothing back on, he picked up the K-Bar knife he had dropped in the hallway earlier during the heat of the pursuit. Then he approached the control room. He entered it, asking for a report. The three remaining men and one woman who hadn't been burned to death earlier said everything was in motion. The final part of the grand plan was near completion.

"Keep your eye on the Gulf of Mexico," Xavier instructed. "Tell me when things start to get *interesting*. I've got other matters to attend to at the moment. Personal matters. *Kill all humans*."

"*Kill all humans*," they parroted.

Xavier made his exit. He re-entered the supply closet nearby for an industrial flashlight and a roll of duct tape. He stood at the peak of the stairway leading into the bottommost level of the cave. They had lost power on that level due to poor electrical work.

No problem, Xavier thought, because the things he wanted to do tonight to Sasha would be more enjoyable in the dark.

He completed the stairs, turned on the flashlight, and began the search for his pretty peach. *Let the games begin*, he thought, cackling into the darkness.

SURROUNDED BY BEASTS

Mack couldn't believe his eyes. He hit the cabin's floor when a series of windows shattered. A dozen or more owls and hawks broke through the glass. As a group, they dug their talons into one of the agent's throats. They peeled through the flesh and tugged on arteries and muscles, until everything from the neck up was a mess of ruptured, upturned pink muscle. The agent's head tipped backwards, striking twice between his shoulder blades, then hanging by a single strand of sinew. The agent's still-gaping mouth coughed up blood and made belching noises until the body finally lost function and toppled over onto the ground.

The other agents blasted their weapons at the birds until the room was covered with flying feathers. Collectively, they shouted in variations of, "What the fuck is going on here?"

One agent was seized through the window by three dogs. Their mouths dug into his back, side, and arm. He was flung legs over head through the window. Mack could hear the ravaging dogs chomp him into raw, bleeding pieces. The man's howls of pain were unbelievable. Stones and the other agent gave each other "Oh shit" expressions.

"What the hell is wrong with nature?" Stones growled. "It's just like those bats at the White House. Green World has turned every animal into a killer. *How is it possible*?"

The other agent kept shaking his head. He couldn't muster any words. Shock was etched into his clammy features. Mack could only stand there and pray nothing ate him.

"*Shhhh*, listen," Stones whispered. "Everybody be quiet a second."

Far off in the woods, sounds of howling, barking, screaming, then gunfire and explosions could be overheard. Mack took it in and realized this was happening everywhere. Then Mack heard the skittering across the roof.

"What the hell is that?" the agent said, standing by the fireplace. "I mean what else is coming after us to fucking kill us?"

The answer came instantaneously.

Fifty-odd squirrels crawled down the chimney and attached themselves to the agent. The man lost himself to fits of terror. He tried to fling the squirrels from his body, but the teeth kept gnashing deeper and deeper into his flesh until they dragged the bloodied agent up the chimney, literally grappling him upwards. Seconds later, the agent was dropped back down into the fireplace piece-by-bloody-piece.

The front door was punched through and slashed into tattered pieces until the barrier was completely removed by a black bear. The species of bear had recently migrated to the area, looking for food. The black-furred beast raged, the hairs on its back rose up sharp as quills.

Stones stepped up, raised his .50 Beowulf assault rifle, and unloaded ten rounds successively. The bear was knocked back into the yard with various gaping holes in its chest.

"Come on, Mack, it's just you and me now! Run to the Land Rover parked out front. I'll get us out of here! Fuck this shit. I'm not anybody's chow!"

Mack's body had gone numb. Agent Stones had to shove him towards the door. "Go! If you want to live, beat your feet."

Mack stumbled through the door. The bear was dead in the front yard. Up in the sky, birds circled overhead like vultures. In the trees, he could hear skittering, chirping, odd snickering, and the clacking of mouths. He wasn't sure what animals lurked around him, but he could see the gleam of their eyes in the darkness.

Snakes were slithering and winding their bodies towards Mack's feet. Field mice and rats were right at their backs, a sight he never thought he'd see in nature! Dogs and cats were working their way towards their positions, each with foaming, champing mouths.

Agent Stones barreled out of the house and tossed an incendiary grenade in three directions. Triple explosions, the arc created a bright ring of fire. That bought them moments to make a move.

"Run to the vehicle, Mack! That's our only chance."

Stones was like an action hero pumping bullets from two .357 Magnums. When those went dry, he un-slung the .50 Beowulf from his back and unleashed more wild gunfire.

Mack entered the passenger side of the Land Rover, and Stones raced over to the driver's side. The vehicle revved up and they were both speeding from the house that had caught on fire from the roaring flames spreading across the yard.

Agent Stones swerved around another black bear, ran over hundreds of snakes, and was charging up the dirt road to an unknown destination.

"Turn on the radio, Mack," the agent demanded. "I want to know if there's any rescue stations, or anything about what the hell is going on here."

Mack tuned in, and immediately turned it off.

Eeeeeeeeeeeeeeeeeeeaaaaaaa!

The whale's song was piercing.

"Damn you, Green World!" Agent Stones shouted. "I get it now. I really do. Kill us all, so they can inherit the world with all the pretty animals. They're killing innocent people. Even their precious animals are getting caught up in the crossfire. That's what happens when smart, capable people become extremists. They do shit that contradicts common sense. They're just crazy, period.

"You have to know something that can help us, Mack. Your daughter was reaching out for help. There has to be some information in that message she texted you that can tell us where they're hiding. Please. It may be the world's only chance."

Mack had Sasha's text memorized.

Dad, I really do love you. It was Xavier. He made me lie. I never hated you. I'm in danger. Mother, she's lost it. They're behind the whale attack. They're planning so much more. We're at that point—

Mack scrutinized every detail, every word, and still, he couldn't come up with anything. He was desperate to help. If nothing was there, he thought, nothing was there.

"I don't know, Agent. I can't read into anything more than what Sasha literally said. I want to help. I wish I had the answer. I swear to you."

"You're going to have to do better than that, Mack. You could be one of those Greenies for all I know. Are you one of those tree-hugging, water-filtering, carbon-footprint reducing assholes?"

"No, I'm not a terrorist! I own a guitar store and give lessons to kids. I'm a pot-smoking, bourbon-drinking, tax-paying idiot! That's what I am!"

"No, Mack. I think you're holding out on me. You want to watch the world bleed to death, is that it? Your group has left you to perish out here and you still stick with them. Nobody will survive in these conditions, and that Goddamn whale! You people are insane. Why have you done this to the world?"

"I'm not one of them, you CIA dick. You know I'm not one of them. You said so yourself earlier."

"That was earlier, but now, I'm not so sure. You're a holdout. You're a Greenie."

"If you call me that one more time, I'm going to strangle you!"

Agent Stones veered to the shoulder, slammed on the brakes, removed the keys from the ignition, and stomped out of the car. They were out in the middle of the woods on a lonely back road. The area was quiet, but Mack wasn't sure for how long it would stay that way.

"You want to strangle me, huh? Here's your chance, you Green bastard. Take your shot."

Mack got out of the car, suddenly terrified of the agent who seemed to have a cool head up against impossible odds, until now.

"I'm not going to fight you. I said that earlier because you're pissing me off. Come on, Agent, we've got bigger problems than who can kick whose ass, am I right?"

"You're wrong, Mack. Kicking your ass would feel real good. My partners are dead, and here you are, alive and well. Getting my knuckles bloody would be downright therapeutic. I might get emotional about it."

"I'm not going along with this macho nonsense. My daughter is clearly in danger. Get it together, man! Think. Be sensible. Brains, not your fists."

Before Mack could say anything else, Stones struck him across the jaw. Mack lost his footing. He landed on his back, sprawled on the ground with a busted, bleeding mouth.

"Get up, you punk. You Greenie! Put your words to action. Strangle me. Kick my ass. Is that all you got? What's with the goofy look on your face, huh? That all you got, you washed up pothead? You ain't talking shit now, Mack. You're pathetic. Say something. Go ahead. Give me a reason to pop you another."

Mack couldn't believe it.

Bizarre wasn't strong enough of a word.

He finally understood what Sasha was trying to tell him in that text.

It made perfect sense.

Why didn't he make the connection earlier?

Mack told Agent Stones what he came up with in that moment. When he was done talking, the agent didn't want to fight him anymore. The agent helped him off of the ground and said, "See, all it took was knocking some sense into you. I guess you're not a Greenie after all. Come on, let's get moving. We might be able to win this war after all."

They piled back into the vehicle, knowing the fight was far from over.

THE FACTS ARE CLEAR

Unbelievable! Everything we predicated to cause the end of the human race and this is what actually does it. A fucking whale. Not solar flares, or economic collapse, or depletion of resources. Green World doesn't know what they've unleashed upon the world. Damn it, why can't we stop them? Why are we so helpless? It's never been this bad.

President Ted Yearling was on his fourth scotch and soda. The room was getting dizzier. The reality of the situation couldn't be avoided, no matter how high his blood-alcohol content. He watched underground in the presidential bunker on the big screens as every country suffered animal attacks. The whale's hypnotic, psychotic song was playing across the Internet, through radio waves, and every communication system across the entire world. Nobody was spared the whale's wrath.

Africa was a bloodbath. Nigeria was knee-deep in ravaged human remains. Russia's streets overflowed with blood. England's Prime Minister was eaten by a pack of savage dogs. The Queen was on a commercial cruiser when a Tiger Shark swallowed the woman whole on the main deck.

Japan and China didn't respond to any communications, whatsoever. France had somehow relayed to them distress messages, but there wasn't any way to reach them. France always found a way to call out for help, the president thought bitterly.

The animals were kamikazes. Birds, bats, and rats would sneak into engines of defensive vehicles, clog them up, and render most flying vessels and military weapons useless. Animals were attacking military bases and camps in rampant numbers. The people were simply outnumbered and out-eaten.

There was no way out of this, President Yearling kept thinking. He was on his next scotch and soda. The president couldn't taste it anymore. His stomach kept sinking. The world was crumbling. His wife and kids were dead. His country was being cut down to ribbons. There was no coming back from this. Green World would inherit the earth.

Because of a whale.

A fucking whale.

The Secretary of Defense was making his rounds about the room and he was about to drop an update on the president. They were throwing ideas at the wall to see what would stick. The problem was, once the walls were slathered in so much gore, nothing else could stick except for more death and despair.

The president didn't want to hear anymore about casualties and devastation. President Yearling stole the Secretary of Defense's Glock from his holster, stuck it in his mouth, and removed the burden of his thoughts. His brains, unlike the United States' defense strategy, did stick to the wall.

SCARED IN THE DARK

Sasha hid in the darkness of the bottommost level of the bunker and waited. The anticipation was the hardest part. She knew Xavier wanted to do bad things to her. The way his evil eyes undressed her. How he changed persona when her mother was around. It was like flipping a light switch. Sociopath. Not a sociopath. Sociopath. Not a sociopath.

She wasn't sure what she was hiding behind. They were cardboard boxes, maybe. Shelves of canned goods. These were all guesses, the room being in such pitch darkness. She backed up into a toolbox. There was a small flashlight inside, among other tools. She grabbed the flashlight and a hammer.

Sasha turned on the flashlight. She had to know what was around her. Xavier hadn't descended the stairs. He had backtracked. The man was getting something to supply his fun with her. It made her gorge rise imagining what made a man like Xavier tick. Everything about the bastard sickened her.

A voice from deep within her mind said, *You can stop him. You can stop everything. You know*

*where the signal's coming from. All you have to do
is kill Xavier. It starts with him being dead.*

It wouldn't be that easy. Xavier had more of his
men guarding the control room. She would have to
get passed all of them to even stand a chance of
terminating the signal that was causing the world's
animals to turn against humanity.

Sasha turned on the flashlight. There were food
and water supplies to last years down here. She
was hiding among aisles and aisles of survival
storage. Sasha kept moving deeper and deeper into
the darkness. She stopped at a desk. It was
Xavier's.

She rummaged through the drawers. She found
lots of documents about Green World. Sasha
gasped at the last file she opened. She read the
typed pages and studied the drawings of a whale
covered in steel. She saw something in bold that
read: BACKUP EMERGENCY CODE: BATTLE
WHALE.

Backup code for what, she wondered.

Sasha kept pouring through the files. There
were studies on human psychology, perception,
radio waves, and mass hypnosis. Green World had
researched and worked on this plan for nearly two
decades. The totality of their agenda was clear.
Nature would reclaim the earth and only the "best"
of humanity would remain here to enjoy the new
world.

You have to stop this.

You're the only one who can.

Sasha kept rummaging through the drawers for
any more information. She happened upon one

document that caused her to reel in horror. There were diagrams, pictures, stats, and general information about another project of Green World's.

Battle Whale #2.

Sasha couldn't believe what she was seeing.

Her eyes were gaping wide.

Chilling laughter echoed from the top of the stairs. Xavier was coming down after her. His voice was a happy child's.

"You're all for me, Sasha. Everything I want to do to you, I will. Don't give up. Fight me, Sasha baby. I like it when they fight back."

Sasha cringed, hearing the sadistic bastard's voice ring off the walls.

She clutched the hammer and flashlight.

If Xavier wanted a fight, so be it.

PART FOUR: WHALE WAR

DEPLOYED

Deep in the ocean, Battle Whale #2 thrashed in its wire cage. The second prototype was connected to a Green World commercial ship disguised as a cruise liner. The vessel sailed in the Gulf of Mexico. The whale's eyes were raging red mechanical cherries. Phase two of Green World's plan was about to enacted. Now that the first battle whale was out of missiles, the second whale would take out new targets in other countries. Long-range missiles would kiss any country's military defenses goodbye.

The locks on the wire cages were disengaged. Battle Whale #2's engines fired up, and the three hundred tons of mammal flew across the ocean to meet up with Battle Whale. Together, their communication signals and #2's firepower would make Green World's plan a sure success.

Green World's elite stood on deck of the commercial cruiser with pride.

The planet would return to nature, and Green World would inherit the earth.

Nothing could stop them now.

HARD RIDE

Agent Stones slammed the gas pedal to the floor, screeching the tires, and burning all hell to reach St. Joseph, Missouri. They had about a two hour drive ahead of them.

"I'm still trying to put together what you told me," Agent Stones said. "You're saying you think Sasha was about to tell you where the signal was coming from right when the text was cut off?"

Mack had turned Sasha's words in his mind time and time again in a mad desperation: *Dad, I really do love you. It was Xavier. He made me lie. I never hated you. I'm in danger. Mother, she's lost it. They're behind the whale attack. They're planning so much more. We're at that point—*

We're at that point—

Sasha was talking about the caves that were a short hike's distance from their old house when Mack was still married to Nora. Mack played some serious games of hide and seek in those caves with his daughter. That was Sasha's favorite place to go, especially when Nora would have bi-polar episodes (undiagnosed at the time), and Mack and Nora would argue heatedly. Mack remembered Nora's surges of anger. She was a ticking time bomb, and she exploded often.

Mack was sad his marriage was beyond repair by the time Nora sought treatment and recovered her mental health, or so he thought she had. Hooking up Xavier had sent her in a new terrible direction altogether, with medication or not.

Agent Stones cut into his thoughts. "So you think the signal's coming from some caves near where you and Sasha used to live?"

"It makes sense. Nora and Xavier still live in that old house near those caves. It's a perfect base for them. I bet they were planning on setting all of this shit into motion, then hiding in those caves, fortifying themselves, then popping back out when everybody was dead except for the animals and other members of Green World. They can hug trees and shovel up dead bodies while singing Kumbaya."

"What if you're wrong? Your daughter's text could've meant several things."

"You got a better plan? So what if I'm wrong? Anything else you were planning to do tonight?"

Agent Stone's expression could've cut through steel. "No plan. It doesn't mean your idea is great. But it's the best we got. Every line of communication is down. I can't contact anybody. Everything's been hijacked by Green World. I guess this is it. If you're wrong, then Green World might just get their way."

The agent was right, Mack thought. This could very well be the end of the world.

Three black bears stood side-by-side in the road ahead of them. They were bent forward, ready to pounce. Mouths were jagged and drooling. They growled and slashed at the air with their claws.

"Strap on your seatbelt, pal," the agent warned. "The trip's going to be a bumpy one."

"You're not going to ram them, are you?"

"No, I'm going to stop the car and ask them to kindly step aside. What the fuck do you think I'm going to do? This is an emergency situation. We either do this, or we kiss everybody's asses goodbye!"

Stones punched the gas, and the Land Rover launched forward. The bear in the middle was thrown up over the windshield, rolled over the top, and dropped down onto the road. The other two bears were pursuing them. The vehicle easily left the bears in the dust.

"Damn, that was crazy!" Mack couldn't believe what was happening. "You just plowed through that bear!"

Agent Stones didn't enjoy the observation. "More trouble up ahead. I want you to take the wheel. I'm going to have to do some shooting. I'm guessing you can't aim worth a damn."

"You'd be right."

After a tricky situation of switching seats, Mack clutched the wheel nervously. The agent worked his way to the back seat. He was opening several weapons cases.

"What do you have back there?"

"Enough to buy us some time. I don't know if it'll be enough, but we might have a chance. You keep the wheel straight, and we'll be just fine."

Mack wasn't emboldened by the agent's words. He could see geese, birds, bats, and owls hover over the vehicle. From the woods, new movement could be detected. Lots of glinting eyes and darting night-obscured bodies. Mack wasn't just nervous; he was trembling everywhere.

He prayed for his daughter and for his theory about the caves to be correct, and for the world to somehow rebound from this awful attack.

Prayers and hopes vanished from Mack's registry.

Steering wheel and fear of death took over Mack's focus.

Agent Stones smashed in the back window. "Time for some shooting gallery fun. Sorry, I left my hunting license at home. Just try and stop me from de-polluting these woods."

"What are you going on about?"

"Let me talk to myself, asshole." Agent Stones had a Winchester pump action 20 gauge shotgun. "Some people piss and shit themselves in these situations, but me, I choose to talk to myself. Still have a problem with the guy saving your ass?"

"You make sure you hit your targets."

"You make sure you drive straight."

Mack was going seventy miles an hour. He was headed towards the main highway, but they had about ten more minutes of driving time in the woods to complete.

The trek was only going to get deadlier with each new mile they traveled.

HIDING FROM A PSYCHOPATH

Sasha wanted to lunge out of the darkness and strike Xavier with a hammer. There were many levels of satisfaction in that idea, and so many risks. She had the flashlight, she reasoned, but to give up her spot before she knew where Xavier was lurking would be a mistake. Xavier was strong. If she tried to strike at the wrong moment, the man would overpower her and have his way with her. The man murdered her mother without missing a beat. Xavier would have zero issues with removing her from this world. But with Xavier, it wouldn't be that simple. It would be brutal, messy, and long-lasting.

The plan was simple, Sasha kept thinking. She would keep moving quietly until she backtracked to the stairs. Sasha could escape this trap and come at him upstairs where she would see her enemy coming from a good distance off.

Xavier made it easy to move about the room.

He wouldn't stop talking.

Or he was bragging, Sasha believed. She could read the most recent edition of the *DSM* guide and still be clueless to the depths of Xavier's depravity.

"You better be nice to me, Sasha, because when this over, when my work with Battle Whale pays off, I'll be king. You want food, you'll have to come to me. You want water, you'll have to drink it from my hands when you're done begging for it on your knees.

"You can be my queen. We're not blood related. It's feasible, Sasha. You're much prettier than your mother. Your body is so much softer. Every part of you is supple and sweet. It's the only comforts I had hiding in that hole. She was your age and she looked just like you, Sasha, when it happened."

What the hell is he talking about?

Sasha stopped moving and listened.

"I have suffered greatly for the cause, long before now. Green World has been around for a very long time. My family, when I was twenty-one, was sent on a mission given to us by Green World. We firebombed a logging company that was taking out giant chunks of the rainforest. Their equipment, their workers, their headquarters, we roasted them all to high hell.

"Our group almost escaped the country without being caught. But the corporate giant behind that logging company tracked us down. We were soon captured. I was separated from my parents and the team. I was tasered into unconsciousness. When I woke, I was at the bottom of a very deep dirt hole. I couldn't climb out, and I certainly couldn't reach the top.

"The hole itself was the size of a finished basement. I thought this billionaire CEO guy had thrown me down there and left me there to die. I wish that was the case. The horrors I experienced were things only hell could provide.

"There was only a tent, a hole for a restroom, and water supplies. They wanted to keep me alive. I soon learned I wasn't alone. Inside that tent, there was a girl named Alana. She was maybe fourteen or fifteen. I met her during the mission. I was twenty-two at the time. It was just me and her to fend for ourselves in this hole.

"We were on the brink of starving to death, when one day, they threw down these things wrapped up in bags. They were sizzling cuts of meat."

Sasha grimaced while hearing this and the rest of Xavier's story.

"We thought nothing of it. We ate the meat, because we were mad with hunger. Up top, we could hear their sick laughter. Alana and I didn't care. We were so very hungry.

"I grew fond of Alana during the time we were in that predicament together. We held each other close during the bitter cold nights to keep warm. We made love, because that was the only comfort we could give each other. That was the only beautiful thing that happened in that dreadful hole.

"The longer we ate this food over the weeks to come, you see, Sasha, we realized the meat was from the members of our team. This became very much obvious when those holding us captives threw down the heads and bones of our friends and family. My mother and father were among those pieces. I had eaten my mother and father. Alana couldn't accept the fact that we'd eaten our friends and family. She took a sharp rib bone and slashed her own throat. Alana was happy to be dead.

"I was left down in that hole to starve, all alone. The people who threw us down in there were long gone. I only had Alana's cold dead body to keep me company. I was determined to escape. I used the assorted human bones as tools to climb out of the deep hole. I eventually caught up with those assholes, and I killed each of them in painful ways.

"I had to research torture techniques, how to keep a person alive with the least amount of organs and limbs. I sutured people together. I turned them into surgical experiments. I had friends who helped me in Green World accomplish this. When they found out what had been done to me, my family, and Alana, and our partners, they wanted in on the action. We eventually left those awful people in a hole of their own piss and shit. They rot as we speak.

"Green World amped up their Battle Whale plan after that. Things were being set in motion very quickly. I returned to the United States and I assumed a new identity, married your mother, the first women I met at the university who could help me re-assimilate into society again. St. Joseph, Missouri, was the perfect base to set up the signal.

"But I saw you, Sasha, and I think of sweet Alana. I can't stop thinking about you, Sasha. You're the sweetest thing. I only want to taste your love. Will you let me taste you?"

Sasha couldn't stand another moment of this lunatic's ramblings.

She lunged out of her hiding spot, swung her hammer, and did everything she could to take out the murdering, lecherous, creepy bastard.

AT THE HELM

Edward Oakley and Robin Flowers were sitting in front of the control panels, upstairs from where Xavier and Sasha were locked in combat. Their job was simple. Guard the controls, maintain the signal being broadcasted, and check in on Battle Whale's status.

The Battle Whale was out of armaments and floated in the Gulf of Mexico underwater. The mass was useless, aside from the radio broadcasts it delivered. Five minutes ago, Battle Whale #2's flight in the sky ended and it dropped back down into the ocean where it's mammalian friend waited.

Battle Whale #2 floated at the ready for word from Green World's secret base for the command to arm its missiles. There were hundreds of new targets to take out. Foreign military defense posts, mostly, that needed to be erased if they were going to start a new peaceful world without violence and animal bloodshed.

"What do you think they'll do with the original Battle Whale now?" Oakley asked Flowers. "It's basically obsolete."

Flowers sighed. "Poor thing will have to be put down, I'm afraid. A whale can't live long-term carrying all that steel. It'll have to be destroyed. Battle Whale #2 is equipped to complete the job in a quick, humane way. Battle Whale won't suffer. She's done us proud."

"You think Battle Whale understands the sacrifice it has to make?"

Flowers smiled. Tears streamed from both of her eyes. "Undoubtedly. Nature has suffered by our hands for far too long. We are preserving our future and extreme measures are required. Losses will be taken on both sides. It's an unfortunate byproduct of progress."

"You're right," Oakley said. "You always had a nice way of saying things. You ever going to finish that book of poetry?"

"When the world's ours, I'll have time to write all the poetry I want."

Oakley and Flowers received word from Green World's main base.

They were to deploy the next series of missile attacks in thirty minutes.

The countdown to total world domination had just begun.

BATTLE WHALE

Floating in the darkness underwater, Battle Whale waited for new orders. The machine's processes echoed throughout the Gulf of Mexico. Battle Whale's song kept projecting from every communication source across the globe. There was nothing left for the colossal mammal to do but to remain in position.

The general calm up against the explosions, screams, and terror spreading about Texas and rest of the United States, was abruptly erased by the thrum of new engines as Battle Whale #2 flew above the water like a mega jet. After unfolding its great wings, terminating its thrusters, and preparing for water landing, Battle Whale #2 splashed down next to the original battle whale.

This whale was sleeker designed, almost a third larger than the original design, and its armaments were fully equipped. A satellite receiver on Battle Whale #2 awaited its command. Any minute, every missile, rocket, and gun would be blazing in the name of Green World.

HIGH-OCTANE SHOOTING GALLERY

Agent Stones was popping off rounds from his .50 Beowulf automatic through the back windshield. A mixture of birds, bats, and deer were collapsing against the road from the powerful blasts. Mack focused on safe driving. He had to get to the main highway and reach St. Joseph, Missouri. Faster and faster, the Land Rover picked up speed. Up ahead, there seemed to be a clearing. They turned off the main exit and entered the highway. Cars were strewn about the roads wrecked, burned up, and abandoned. Mack had to angle around each vehicle. Many were parked on the shoulder. Victims had been pulled out of shattered car windows, dragged out onto the pavement, and devoured.

Six black and white cows were chewing on piles of strewn human corpses like they would grass. When they passed the cow's buffet line, Stones left them five grenades as dinner mints.

"Looks like there's going to be a lot of causalities," Stones said, sniping a crow who was trying to wedge an eyeball from a dead woman's socket. The crow disintegrated. "Who knows how many will survive this tragedy?"

Mack refused to digest the dark thought. There had to be others alive. The world couldn't end this way. There had to be a—

A beaver had clutched onto the side mirror and was bashing its paw against the window to reach Mack. It bared its sharp teeth, hurling foam onto the glass.

"Reach under your seat, Mack. There's a nice .357. Go ahead and take it out before it gets the same idea about you!"

Mack scrambled for the gun. He reached with two of his longest fingers and he barely grazed the handle.

The beaver slammed its head into the glass, once, twice, three times, before the glass gave to the blows. Glass sprayed Mack. The beaver's claws raked down the meat of Mack's forearm. The beaver was about to clutch onto his arm and climb up his extremity for the throat when Mack jammed the nozzle of the pistol into its face and let loose three thundering rounds. The beaver's body was no more.

Mack's arm was leaking blood. He reached into the other seat, grabbed a spare t-shirt, and tied it around the wound. Before he could say that was a close one, up ahead, the highway was covered in rats. Thousands of them! Their collective hiss drew sharp gooseflesh on Mack's body.

"We're in for it now!"

Agent Stones vocalized a gut check. "Fuck that noise. *They're* in for it now. Drive on. We're heroes, whether you like it or not."

A rabbit was flying at the vehicle as if thrown and Mack stuck the .357 out of the car and blasted it mid-air. It popped into pink confetti-gut streamers. After that, the hordes of rats were charging full-on. The tires crunched, popped, and exploded many of them. Others were crawling up the doors and trying to sneak into the vehicle.

Mack punched and slapped many of the rats off of the open window. He sped up, driving wildly back and forth between lanes to shake them off. Rats covered the hood and they were pressing against the windshield. Heads, tiny fists, and bodies were banging against the glass Spider cracks turned into artery-sized cracks. Then suddenly the windshield gave with a wild explosion of jagged flying pieces. Mack slowed the car, unbuckled his seat belt, and crawled over the seats to the very back. The rats were coming in!

Agent Stones had already escaped through the back windshield. The agent scrambled to help Mack escape by the same route as rats tore up the seats in their fury to reap human flesh.

One of the rats turned on the dial to the radio and the disconcerting whale's song played out on speakers:

Eeeeeeeeeeeeeaaaaaaaaaa!
Eeeeeeeeeeeeeaaaaaaaaaa!
Eeeeeeeeeeeeeaaaaaaaaaa!

"Run, for fuck's sake, run!" The agent retreated up the highway and Mack struggled to follow in his wake. Agent Stones had to abandon his .50 and was now blasting two Ruger pistols at anything coming their way.

Three geese tried to swoop down and peck at Mack, but before they could reach him, they were reduced to pieces by the agent's bullets.

"Pick it up, Keever," Stones commanded. "We've got to find a vehicle. It's no good on foot."

"We've got a wide selection of vehicles here on Highway 50," Mack said. "Take your pick. Each one comes with a half-eaten body or two. We'll call it the "blood and guts" sale."

Soooooooooooooonk!

A giant flying object careened across the highway and smashed into a garbage truck. The entire thing left the ground and went up into flames. The incoming rats were aflame, some popping from the heat and instantly turning into vapor.

Deer with bloodied antlers were charging in at them next, backed up by a sky assault of wild geese, blue jays, robins, and cardinals. Their death cheeps filled the night air.

Soooooooooooooonk!
Soooooooooooooonk!
Soooooooooooooonk!

Three more shots obliterated a quarter mile's radius of highway. Enemies on foot and in the sky were wiped out in a blaze of incendiary glory. For three seconds, it rained chunky blood.

Mack searched and soon spotted the RV parked ahead of them. There was a man standing on top of it who was re-loading a new round into his rocket launcher. He was a pot-bellied guy dressed in a denim jacket, denim pants, and a confederate flag dew rag. The stranger shouted at them, "FUCK YEAH. AMERICA AIN'T GOIN' OUT SO EASILY! I'M SENDING YOU STRAIGHT TO HELL IF YOU CROSS ME!!!"

Large snakes crawled up the side of the RV, slithered up his body, crawled, and pried their way into his mouth. His cheeks puffed out. The man's neck bulged until it popped from the internal pressure. The snakes shoved out his eyeballs while making their exit.

"Hurry," Agent Stones shouted. "We can commandeer that vehicle. I bet the dead fool left the keys in the ignition."

Mack struggled to carry himself forward that much faster, but thinking about Sasha and her message of distress, he dug so deep and found that extra push he needed to reach the vehicle. Stones was blasting his weapons to scare off the snakes crawling on the RV.

Mack opened the car to find a snarling mad opossum bare its teeth at him in the driver's seat.

"I'm in no mood!"

Mack picked up the opossum and punted it high up into the air and away from the vehicle. He piled into the RV, threw the door shut, and when Agent Stones met him inside, the agent was more than pleased. Small arms, high-powered shotguns, rifles, and machine guns lined the floor by the dozens.

"The asshole up top must've been a doomsday prepper, or a conspiracy theorist, or a Southern madman. I don't who he was, but he's dead now, and we've hit the mother load."

Mack had good news to report as well.

The keys were in the ignition.

Mack fired up the RV and continued what they had started.

Their guns never stopped blazing.

LASHING OUT

Sasha had to guess where to aim the hammer when she swung it down on Xavier. Her calculations were right on the money. The hammer clapped over the crown of the skull. Xavier let out a yelp of surprise and pain. The man required more than a knock over the head because his strong, burly arms suddenly wrapped tightly around her body.

"So soft, so sweet," he whispered in her ear. "Comfort me like Alana did, sweet Sasha. You smell so good."

"You really are IN-SANE!"

Sasha head-butted him on the nose. The man clutched both hands over his blood- burbling nose. When Sasha landed on the ground, she immediately started running towards the stairs. Lunging up to the next level, Sasha realized she still clutched the hammer in her hand.

She closed in on the two guards outside the control room. The one guard was caught by surprise by the wild screaming girl lunging at him with a hammer. The guard reached for his sidearm with bulging, shocked eyes. Before he could get his hands on the 9mm, Sasha clubbed him over the head three times. The first two blows had him seeing stars; the third blow had him seeing death. Sasha swung the hammer at the other guard, killing him instantly with one single crack.

She tried to open the control room door. She could kill the signal and disarm battle whale. The attack against the world could end.

The door was locked.

Damn it.

She lowered down to the guard on the floor nearest to her. Sasha rooted through his pockets, his belt, and located a key ring.

Sasha had twelve keys to try.

The first two keys were useless.

Xavier was trudging his way up the stairs. He had his 9mm extended in his right arm. Before he could fire, Sasha drew the pistol from the dead guard's holster and emptied two rounds into Xavier. He faltered to the ground and lay unmoving where he fell.

"Die, you bastard."

She tried the next key. It was the right one.

When Sasha plowed through the door, a gun was already trained on her.

The stand-off would end in blood.

XAVIER

Xavier had a bullet lodged in his left shoulder and another somewhere in his lower torso. No matter the bullet's location, it all added up to internal bleeding. There wasn't a doctor who could help him. He would have to remove the bullet himself, pray he could stop the bleeding, but first, he had to preserve the mission. Green World couldn't fail; not after coming this far.

He forced himself up from the ground.

Blood spilled in his wake.

By now, the second phase of the mission had been engaged. Battle Whale #2 was set to unleash another missile attack on strategic points throughout the world. Defense bases, arm's storage, and rescue and aid operations would be reduced to nothing.

Nature would inherit the earth and Green World would shoulder the burden of creating a new humanity. But first, Sasha had to be stopped. Then he would have fun with her body.

Xavier could hear gunshots in the control room.

Maybe he wouldn't have to do anything to stop her. He had good solid people working with him on this mission. Good people to take back the world from evil.

Xavier tried the control door, but it was locked.

He pounded, and pounded, and pounded on the door, and still, nobody opened it from the other side.

Xavier knew then what kind of trouble the mission was in so he opened fire on the door. He was getting through to the other side no matter what, and when he did, Sasha better watch out. The bitch was going to get it just like her mother did.

KEEP ON RU'ING

Mack clutched the wheel of the RV and watched the highway up ahead of him with maximum scrutiny. They enjoyed a moment where things seemed to clear up, but that ended shortly. Hawks were swooping in with rats clutched in their talons. They dropped them down onto the RV. Rats chewed and raked their nails against the roof to reach them. Mack used a cigarette lighter to burn one and Stones was shooting a Desert Eagle pistol to turn them into microwave-wall spatter.

Behind them, an assortment of deer, bears, dogs, cats, horses, and goats were charging in at them. Mack lifted up a Gatling gun and unleashed a bullet hell upon them. Hundreds of rounds were unleashed on the savage pack of animals.

"Yeah, eat it!"

Mack knew they were thirty minutes from reaching the turn-off. They would enter a small town called Dog Wood and take a series of back roads that lead into thick woods. They would have to hit the trail and hike to the local cave systems.

They could be wasting their time. Mack's theory about Sasha's message could be a dead end.

Agent Stones had emptied the Gatling gun and was unleashing a wall of M-16 fire into more raging animals. The agent had gone through over a dozen weapons before they arrived to the exit leading into Dog Wood.

"Hold on," Mack said. "I'm exiting. We're almost there."

The agent couldn't hear a word Mack had said.

The guns were much too loud.

CONTROL ROOM

Sasha didn't give the guard in the control room a chance to consider the situation. She unleashed two bullets into the man's heart, hitting him center mass. The woman at the control panel, Flowers, didn't reach for her gun.

She spoke warnings.

"You can't stop us. Battle Whale #2 is three minutes from unleashing its missile attack on strategic points in the world. We will cripple the world's defenses. We are the final straw that breaks the backs of nations. You're fighting for a useless cause. The world is ours, you stupid little girl! Go ahead, kill me, you—"

Sasha shot her in the head.

"Fine. Have it your way."

Sasha nudged the corpse out of the chair with brains leaking out of her head and took helm of the controls. She had stood beside her mother and Xavier in this room many times before. Sasha had an extensive understanding of the controls and their functions. Her time hiding from Xavier downstairs had steered her in the directions of the proper files that could save the world from total human extinction.

She had the code to unleash Battle Whale's emergency attack. It might not take out Battle Whale #2, but it bought the world time. If it was all she could do for now, then so be it.

First, Sasha terminated the animal brainwashing signal. Then she accessed Battle Whale's terminal. She entered Battle Whale's emergency code and a new screen flashed on the panel. Her options were limited.

Battle Whale Terminate Plan
Battle Whale Emergency Attack Mode
Battle Whale Mission Abort

Sasha couldn't abort the mission. On the left terminal's screen, she could see two whales floating in the Gulf of Mexico. One appeared to be aimless, without any weapons, and the second whale, was loaded up to the brim with missiles and rockets from top to bottom.

Sasha had two minutes before the next wave of attacks was unleashed. She had no control over Battle Whale #2. Another tower somewhere else full of evil assholes had the reigns over that sea creature.

Sasha racked her brains to make a decision. How could she save the world in two minutes?

Battle Whale Terminate Plan
Battle Whale Emergency Attack Mode
Battle Whale Mission Abort

Sasha engaged Battle Whale's Emergency Attack Mode. The screen asked her what target to terminate.

Sasha typed, then hit enter: **Battle Whale #2.**

Right after she did that, bullets were fired into the door. The gun only had two bullets. She heard the firearm click, dry. Xavier cursed, then let loose his diabolical thoughts, "LET ME IN RIGHT NOW!"

Xavier's eyes peeked into the room through one of the bullet holes. The orb penetrated her where she sat. Sasha could see his eyes zoom in on her.

Then he cackled, "I'm getting in there. I still have my K-bar knife. I'm going to enjoy you from the inside out. Have it your way. We do this the hard way."

Sasha heard him stagger to another end of the hall.

He soon returned, bashing a fire extinguisher against the wood.

She didn't know how much longer the door would hold.

EERIE SILENCE

Mack geared up for more flesh-eating animals and even more artillery destruction. What he didn't expect was a sudden calm to overtake the night. Along the streets, in smashed up businesses, animals stopped feasting on human flesh. Mack was disturbed by the Border Collie with red smearing its face stare off in the distance as if confused. Wild animals were flying up in the sky, returning to the woods, and ending their reign of terror.

"I don't get it," Stones said, putting down his weapons and coming up to the passenger seat. "The animals…just stopped."

Mack thought of something. "I'm flipping on the radio. I have to check this out."

The whale's song didn't play on the waves. An emergency broadcast was repeating, telling those alive to stay in shelter until local aid groups could assemble. Mack kept flipping through the channels. They were repeats of the same emergency message, except for one rogue signal.

"PEOPLE OF THE WORLD. THE FINAL BATTLE IS UPON US. IT'S HAPPENING NOW IN THE GULF OF MEXICO. BATTLE WHALE

VS. BATTLE WHALE. I'M SEEING IT HAPPEN LIVE FROM THE SHORELINE. THE ONLY HOPE FOR HUMANITY. GOD HELP US. I CAN'T BELIEVE WHAT I'M SEEING!"

Mack wasn't sure what the madman shouting into the microphone was going on about. Stones scanned the channels. Mack kept driving to reach their destination. After listening to six different persons reporting on the whales, they were able to put the facts together.

"I don't know how a weapon-less whale is going to take on a fully-armed whale," Mack said, disbelieving the words that were coming out of his mouth. "Somebody on the right side must be trying to undo Green World's mess."

"Whoever it is, they better know what they're doing," Stones snarled. "If that whale unleashes those missiles, we could all be in trouble. I'm talking scorched earth everywhere."

Mack drove as far as he could out on several back roads. They reached a park called Briar Wood Park. Mack explained they would have to take it on foot to reach their cave system. This was the direct-most route.

Mack hurried out of the vehicle and made a run for it. Stones stayed behind.

"Come on, my daughter could be in danger!"

"I'm not going anywhere unarmed. Neither should you."

"You got a point. Load me up."

Agent Stones and Mack armed themselves and they stormed into the woods in search of the cave system.

XAVIER'S PLIGHT

Xavier had blood trickling down his right side and left arm. He didn't care. He was getting into that control room! Xavier clutched onto a fire extinguisher and beat it against the door. After three strikes, he required a moment to catch his breath. The blood loss had him dizzy.

He decided to appeal to Sasha.

Maybe he could convince her to open the door.

"You engaged emergency battle mode, didn't you?" Xavier raised his voice so it would reach Sasha. "And I noticed you turned off the animal signal. You think you're a hero, Sasha? You think you saved humanity? You're one of us, little girl. You've helped the cause. Your hands are dirty. They'll hang you for this, or will it be the electric chair?"

He wasn't getting anything out of Sasha.

She stayed quiet.

Xavier tried a new approach.

"I see this going down one of two ways. I do nothing. I stand here and bleed in this hallway. Battle Whale gets destroyed by Battle Whale #2. Nothing changes. Nature will inherit the world. I turn on the animal signal, I watch those missiles be deployed, and I die knowing Green World's mission succeeded. Then I kill you.

"Or how about this option? I much prefer this idea too, by the way. You help me. Patch me up. You make it up to me, Sasha, in only the way a very young woman can. I'll go slow. I know you're a virgin. Making love can be a sweet thing. Give me a chance, Sasha. We both watch Green World's plan as intended, and we move on from this misunderstanding. Now how about opening the d—"

Sasha growled, "How about *my* plan, Xavier? You bleed to death out there, and I save the world. I wouldn't let you near me in any capacity. Now shut the fuck up so I can undo the damage you've created."

Xavier absorbed her abrasive words. Sasha was nothing like her mother.

This would require another course of action.

Xavier's mind conspired.

RADIO COMMUNICATION

Sasha was trembling from her head down to her feet. Xavier remained a cold and chilling presence behind the door. He gave up any attempts to batter down the door, for the meantime. She wasn't sure if he lurked nearby, of if he'd relocated to another part of the bunker. She couldn't hear his labored breathing anymore. Maybe he died.

I'm not that lucky, she thought. *Keep focusing on the problem at hand.*

She punched into the system for the Battle Whale to go into its emergency mode. She waited for any reaction from the machine. Sasha studied the control panel and she happened upon a radio channel. She turned it on and spoke into the small microphone installed into the computer. Sasha wasn't sure who'd hear her words, or if they would matter, but she spoke them anyway.

"If anybody's listening, I've terminated the signal that's causing the animals to kill people. I've infiltrated Green World's base in St. Joseph, Missouri. I'm in a cave at Briar Wood Park. Please send help. I'm doing what I can to stop either whale from harming anyone else. All I can do is try my best. I'm sorry for the harm this organization has caused this world. I never wanted anything bad to happen to anyone. I can only hope Battle Whale can stop this other whale from deploying its missiles. I pray we can rebuild the world, as it is."

Sasha wasn't sure what else to say.

She signed off after repeating her location and begging for help.

Sasha studied the screen again.

Battle Whale was engaged. Now all she could do was watch, and wait.

Xavier's voice was a faint whisper. It still harbored the potent chill. She imagined a little bit of the darkest, deepest pit of his soul escaped between each syllable he delivered from his deviant lips. Sasha turned to see his mouth up against one of the bullet holes in the door. She could see the cherry-colored blood staining his teeth. Xavier was holding back, but soon, very soon, he would unleash his intentions upon her.

"*There she is,*" he whispered in a twisted sing-song voice. "*There she is. Oh, there she is, sitting in that room all alone. There she is.*

"I'm coming in, Sasha," Xavier's voice was now cool and crisp. The confidence had returned to the psycho. He wasn't in pain, or struggling to breathe. "I've stopped the bleeding. After taking some drugs, the pain has gone away. Good for me. *God-awful for you.*"

The sing-song returned.

"*Bing cherries. Cordial cherries. Black cherries. Maraschino cherries. I never met a cherry I couldn't pop.* If I can't pop yours, sweet Sasha, then I'll cut it up WITH MY AXE!!!"

Sasha screamed when Xavier drove his weapon into the door. She saw the triangular steel shape of the axe's head breach her side. It reflected the light for two seconds before Xavier yanked back and drove the axe again, and again, and again.

With the murderous energy Xavier was wielding, the door would in pieces in no time at all. Sasha could only wait in horror at her incoming demise.

COMMENCE BATTLE

Battle Whale's emergency battle systems were engaged. Along its body, engine thrusters kicked on. Fuel cells were energized. Weapons were checked. Rockets: 0. Machine gun bullets: 0. Napalm: 0. Special defenses: 0. Emergency defenses: Fully Functional. Battle Whale's radar scanned the gulf, and it set its sights on Battle Whale #2. Before it could lock target, #2 sent a stream of torpedoes its way. Four of the five torpedoes went wide when Battle Whale pivoted to the right. One torpedo exploded, sheering its left steel wing from its body. Battle Whale's wound was sealed up by liquid metal and patched up in five seconds. All fires were extinguished instantly.

#2 surged towards its enemy, its red mechanical eyes glowing evil. From both sides of the beast, machine gun turrets unleashed ten thousand bullets in fifteen seconds. The shields along Battle Whale's belly was lifted up by steel arms. The barriers blocked the bullets from hitting home. Steel pinged and shed sparks, absorbing what should've shredded the whale into bits.

Battle Whale retaliated the only way it could. It swam head-on towards its enemy, swung its body back, whipped its tail, and steel collided against steel. #2's topmost missile cannons were stripped from its body. #2 unleashed three missiles that painted the water an oil black, buying it time to recover its systems.

Battle Whale didn't relent.

Its rocket thrusters unleashed a powerful blast of force and propelled it onwards yet again to continue the fight.

Jimmy Hatfield was huddled together with his family in the basement of his New Jersey home. He hugged his wife close to his body. Jimmy then brought in his son and daughter for an embrace. Together, they were enthralled by the current radio feed. The wild voice from the rogue broadcast gave a play-by-play of the whale's fight.

Jimmy whispered, "*God be with Battle Whale.*"

The new Prime Minister of England, Blair Chutney, was passing out aid supplies throughout the broken city of London. This section had suffered the worst from the missile and animal attacks. Police cars surrounding the town square were playing the radio broadcast from giant speakers. Body bags were being loaded up. Streets were being cleaned of blood. Those missing were being searched by volunteer patrols.

Blair listened in on the broadcast and said, "*You're our last chance, Battle Whale. You can't fail the world.*"

Battle Whale faced the obscuring oily curtain and didn't hold back. Around its body, openings and slots produced panels of steel. Battle Whale prepared to become a battering ram. Before the steel panels could fall into place, a rocket struck Battle Whale's chest. Engulfed in flames, the burst threw Battle Whale over the surface of the water. Battle Whale hit the shoreline. It lay there vulnerable in the sand, unable to get back into the water.

#2's rockets were aimed at the sky.

Sixty seconds and counting for deployment.

Harold Mosley stood at the head of the Mormon Church in Lowville, Utah. The congregation of two-hundred and thirty were listening in on the broadcast. When everybody heard Battle Whale was beached, Harold motioned for his followers to drink the wine in the goblets in front of them. In less than a minute, everybody went unconscious, then dead. Harold could hear the collective beating of their hearts cease.

Harold threw back his glass of wine.

The last thing he heard on the radio was: *Battle Whale remains beached! There is no hope for humanity's survival!*

The children of Paris drew on the sidewalks with multiple colors of chalk. They were all creating the same image: a whale. Adults wrote message on the sidewalks saying goodbye to the world and final messages to the ones they loved.

Some were words of hope, others celebrations of life, while some were grim epitaphs. For those with a bird's eye view of Paris, the hope of survival never left the faces of the children as they drew Battle Whale somehow toiling on to victory.

Judd Checkers, the seventy-five year old coot Missouri-man, threw back another swig of moonshine. His wife, Myrtle, and his two sons, Jack and Jake, were holed up in the basement getting high on meth. Judd didn't mind the meth, but not now, not when so much was on the line. He wasn't a man of God and he wasn't a man of hope, and he wasn't much of a man at all these days, having busted his ass in a steel factory until he retired with a broken body and a broken heart a year ago. He had suffered the idiocy of his children, the infidelity of his wife, drug and alcohol addiction, but one thing he wouldn't suffer, and that was a bunch of hippies destroying the world.

Judd remained glued to the rogue radio broadcast.

He fired up the propane lantern, smoked a cigarette, enjoyed more of his moonshine, and listened to the battle rage on. It wasn't until the next update that Judd came alive, and shouted, *"Come on, you fuckin' whale! Get off that beach and start kickin' sum ass!"*

"We can't let it end like this. We can't. You're just going to stand by and let the world end? No. Not me. I won't allow it."

Neil Lowman, the man in his mid-forties wearing a Red Socks baseball cap, stood among the many who surrounded the shoreline of the battle ground. Neil refused to stand there and stare at Battle Whale flounder against the sand.

His wife, Elizabeth, didn't agree. "What are you going to do, Neil? Push it back out onto the water. Idiot. You never think things through."

Neil took Elizabeth's disdain and ran with it in a positive direction.

"You know what? That's exactly what I'm going to do. Watch me, bitch!"

Neil charged downhill, stomped through the remains of the destroyed pier, the nasty death pieces created by the killer crabs earlier this evening and stopped in front of Battle Whale. The noises it made were of sheer desperation.

Those black eyes appealed to Neil.

They begged for help.

"Don't worry, big guy. We'll get you back out there fighting in no time."

Neil pushed, and pushed, and pushed against its back. It was useless. One man's force was nothing up against the mega-ton beast.

Neil called out to those up on the hill.

"SOME HELP HERE! Think about where we came from. There will always be somebody in our way. Someone's always going to be jealous or envious of what you got and will do anything to destroy it. Let's stand up for what's good in our lives. You going to fold over and give up, or are you going to rage on tooth and nail? This isn't what my ancestors died for. If you want your life, if you want your freedom back, you're going to have to help me push this whale back into the ocean!"

#2 aimed its rockets to the sky.
The thirty second countdown began.
Battle Whale remained beached.

Neil refused to give up. He wasn't going to stand by and watch hell go down. This wasn't the way he was raised. The American ideals were bullshit. Morality was crap. Humanity was crap. Everything was crap. But nobody was going to dictate when he was to roll over and die. That much he could control.

Neil kept pushing, shoving, grunting, growling, plowing, and applying his might into saving the world. He was startled when the whale started to move.

Everybody on the hill had joined him.

The group had moved the whale two inches on the shore. Nowhere close to where it needed to be. Neil cussed, threw his baseball cap aside, and then was blasted twelve feet back, doing a forced back flip, when Battle Whale's sand-blocked engine came to life. They had budged the whale enough to clear its engine.

The whale sprang up off the sand, launched into the air, and the whale flew back into the ocean.

When everybody dusted off the rattled Neil, he could only watch with wide eyes and a concussed head as the fight between the two whales commenced.

NO HOPE

Battle Whale crashed into #2's side, slamming it back into the water with its battering ram force. #2's target locks were ruined. Both whales were regaining their bearings from the powerful collision. #2 was quicker regaining function and unleashed a powerful throng of machine gun fire. Battle Whale's back took hundreds of rounds of damage, some piercing through its armor and reaping blood. Battle Whale unleashed another round of emergency defenses. From its belly, saw blades poked out with jagged teeth. With a nitrous explosion of speed, Battle Whale's engines rocketed towards the whale and sliced #2's right wing clean off. #2 retaliated with a series of grenade harpoons that blew up the rows of saw blades. Two more missiles blew up Battle Whale's right two engines, leaving only two functional. The third engine conked out when another round of machine gun fire caused too much fuel to leak out and for its hind quarters to catch on fire.

Battle Whale was spinning head-first, unable to right itself, or stop its descent, towards the bottom of the sea. The whale was covered in flames and losing vital functions by the second. Battle Whale's lights went dark and disappeared into the abyss.

#2 returned to its position on the surface and re-locked missiles on its prime targets.

A new countdown began.

This time, nothing could stop the destruction.

SASHA AT THE HELM

Sasha couldn't believe it. The whale's systems were terminated. The screen went dark. There were no further options. Battle Whale was as good as dead. Nothing could be salvaged from this rescue mission.

A message was relayed to her on the computer screen. It came from an unknown location. They identified themselves as a Green World representative.

"*Nice try. Your whale is nothing against ours. Kiss your ass goodbye. Your efforts were for nothing. See you in hell. We're working on turning back on the animal signal. You've prevented nothing. Green World forever.*"

Sasha refused to give up. She searched the computer screen for options, punched numbers, searched the defensive databases, and tried anything and everything to bring life back to Battle Whale. There was only one thing she could try to do.

Sasha turned off Battle Whale's system and rebooted its computer.

Xavier kept heaving his axe into the wood. Bits and pieces were flying into the room. Xavier punched a square through a weak spot, reached through, and opened the door. Xavier kicked open the barrier, clutched the axe in both hands, and eyed her like a thing to defile.

"You're all mine. I have you. There's nowhere you can run. My little cherry. I want to taste you. I want you to pop in my mouth."

"Taste this, prick!"

The fist sent Xavier reeling across the room. He went head-first into the wall. Xavier, slithered to the floor, stunned.

"Dad!"

Mack hugged his daughter. "Did this guy hurt you?"

"No. You saved me." She stared at Agent Stones. "Who's this guy? And how did you get into the base?"

Mack smiled. "It's a long story. Let's just say we tracked you down by the text you sent me. We had to survive some crazy shit to get here. Agent Stones bypassed the code entry into the cave. This was hard to find. Everything's nice and camouflaged. It didn't stop us. Nothing did."

Xavier raised the axe and said, "I'm going to slit you open from your pretty hole up to your pretty pink lips, you—"

Agent Stones shot him twice in the skull.

"I just met that guy, and everything I've heard about Xavier has been confirmed. He's a psycho. Now a dead psycho, that is."

Agent Stones ran to the control panel. He began typing furiously at the console. Sasha and Mack joined him.

"What are you going to do?" Sasha asked. "I've tried everything to get Battle Whale back online."

Agent Stones played around with the system. "One last ditch effort. Watch this, guys. I'm going to light the night up!"

Stones typed in the world's last hope.

They watched the screen in painful anticipation.

They could only pray Battle Whale responded.

HOLD ON

The Secretary of Defense had finished the terrible job of scooping up President Yearling's brains from the floor and plopping them into a bucket. He dumped the brains in the trash, tied the bag off at the top, and cleaned himself up in a corner sink.

The president's brains always belonged in the trash.

Idiot couldn't balance the budget, how could he save us from this?

The Secretary of Defense talked to members of the president's cabinet, the vice-president, and tried to get a hold on the situation. The think tank beneath the White House was a waste. Nobody had solutions to the problem.

The Secretary of Defense eyed the screen on the wall. They had a view of the Gulf of Mexico. Battle Whale had long since sank down into the ocean. They had little time before the missile attack was launched. The Secretary imagined if that happened, there wouldn't be much left of the world to salvage. The earth would die screaming in peril.

The Secretary hung his head down and wept.

There wasn't a damn thing he could do to save the world.

Maybe he would blow out his brains too.

* * *

The New York Philharmonic choir had assembled themselves in Times Square. They were singing songs of hope and peace. The notes spread about the city and everybody remained glued to the radio broadcast with eyes and ears in total thrall.

Neil Lawton, and everybody else on the shore, began throwing rocks, chunks of concrete, and other debris at #2 as its rockets aimed upwards at the sky.

Neil refused to give up hope.

Somehow, good would triumph over evil.

Beverly Hills had been decimated by animal attacks. Among those who remained alive was Lisa Black, a proud Goth, who was holed up in Spank's Tattoo Parlor. Her new boyfriend, Freddy Rotten, was working on a tattoo. They listened to the rogue radio broadcast together as Freddy tattooed Battle Whale on Lisa's left butt cheek. Together, they chanted the words "Battle Whale" over and over again.

Duke Plumber had just finished burying his wife and kids in his backyard. They had been torn to pieces by the cattle on his farm. Horned, stomped, gutted, and ravaged, to be exact. Duke hadn't buried *bodies*. He had buried *pieces*.

His radio played updates on the whale battle.

Duke could give a damn. Take the world, because what he loved best had already been taken from him.

"You can fucking have it, whales! Go ahead and take it!"

Duke enjoyed a swig of whiskey, toasted the sky, then flipped off the sky.

"Go shove a whale up your butt, God! No, shove TWO whales up your butt!"

Every citizen in downtown Detroit walked the streets carrying banners, flags, and signs displaying words of hope, courage, and drawings of Battle Whale. The parade-goers held hands, and did their best to keep their hope in the future of humanity alive.

Fireworks were blasted in the yards throughout cities in the Midwest. Guns were fired into the sky. Booze, final goodbyes, and last minute goodbye fucks were enjoyed by virgins, bold Mennonites, school teachers, and old friends throughout the world. Humanity prepared for the end in high style, because they knew the end was indeed at hand.

The Secretary of Defense looked up at the screen. He dried his eyes with both sleeves in a hurry. Everybody in the White House bunker was on high alert. Deep in ocean, two red eyes blazed bright like two struck road flares.

Battle Whale was back.

FINALE

#2 was thirty seconds from launching a world-wide missile attack. All systems were go. Targets were locked. The rocks and debris hitting its steel exterior from those angry individuals on the shoreline did nothing to halt the attack.

Green World would win the fight.

Sasha patted Agent Stone's back.

"Battle Whale's up and running. What did you do?"

Agent Stones smiled at Mack and Sasha. "Oh, you'll see."

Louis Parker, the voice behind the rogue radio broadcast, was sailing on his yacht. He retired from being a director of advertising for Lamborghini two years ago and pursued his hobby, being a radio show personality. He enjoyed telling humorous stories about people, society, and their bullshit. Louis's voice was a boisterous hybrid of the late sports commentator Harry Carey. Now, he was the mouthpiece of the whale war.

He saw it happen and announced to the world the battle was back on:

"DON'T KISS THE WORLD GOOBYE JUST YET. WHOOOOAYEEEEEAH! WHAT'S BATTLE WHALE DOING? I CAN'T BELIEVE WHAT MY EYES ARE SEEING! THIS IS INSANE!!!"

#2's scans sensed Battle Whale surging up from the sea. Missiles remained on prime targets. Twenty seconds from deployment and counting. The upgraded whale set its defenses to halt Battle Whale's efforts.

Battle Whale was a ravaged, half turned inside out bulk of circuitry, mechanical guts, and real whale guts. It was shedding layers of steel, empty fuel cells, battery cells, and useless cannons. Any extra weight was ditched. One engine remained functional, propelling its body up at gradually building speeds. Every remaining bit of nitrous was injected into that one engine and the beast traveled at over a hundred miles an hour, and still increasing pace. Without weapons, and so very near total collapse, Battle Whale had one final act of war to finish.

#2 was surrounded in burning pools of fire. It set the protective ring to deter its incoming enemy. Liquid napalm turned the vicinity into a boiling concoction of skin-burning stew. Floating bomb buoys were spread out to explode its enemy. A soot-thick curtain obscured visibility from the powder it had sprayed into the air. Cannons were set to shred whatever sprung up from the water into garbage disposal fodder. #2's missiles were set to blast off into the sky.

Twelve seconds and counting.

Total decimation.

* * *

Battle Whale's censors were scrambled by the noxious concoction of napalm and flames. Its skin was boiling like bacon, popping and tearing off in greasy strands. Machinery shorted out, unleashing sparks, then totally going black. Its bulk tripped a buoy bomb, exploding its belly in a shower of guts and chewed up metal. Another buoy bomb, two more buoy bombs, it was like a cleaver had chopped its body into four smoking hot portions. Its entire body from the neck down to the back fin was disintegrated. The head was all that remained. At its neck, a new engine roared, coughing out a giant bloom of flames from its hybrid exhaust pipe. A severed whale head catapulted itself from the surface so insanely fast, vapor trails spread for a quarter of a mile. Battle Whale's final strike was about to be unleashed.

Sasha could see Battle Whale's vital signs.

The whale was just a flying head!

Her question, more like an accusation, was directed at Agent Stones. "What have you done? Was this your plan?"

"I said watch!" Stones snapped.

Mack held Sasha close.

All three waited in unbearable anticipation.

Louis Parker reported the explosions and couldn't help but state what was on his mind. "Battle Whale can't survive those conditions. Nothing can. Even the whale on the surface is starting to melt. I don't know what to say, my fellow survivors. Our hopes have been strung out to the point there is none left. I won't lie. Humanity is facing its final curtain. We're all doomed to die. We're all, huh, wait, what was that? FUCK ME IN THE JESUS HOLE! WHAT THE HELL IS THAT? GO BATTLE WHALE!!!"

Surging from the surface of the sea, its whale flesh and steel coating faceplate were slowly dissolving to skull. The projectile whale head kept plowing forward, propelled by wicked bursts of engine flames and the force and power of a rocket.

Battle Whale's mouth opened, and opened, and opened, widening and widening, until the mouth was big enough to swallow up its enemy. Steel jagged teeth spread along its bone jaws capable of chewing up cars and junking the biggest of rigs. The compactor mouth gave one test chomp, reaping sparks between the eighty jagged death teeth. It happened in three seconds. Battle Whale's mega-mouth clamped shut like a bear trap over #2's head. Three rapid chomps, and #2 was decapitated. The fourth chomp, it clamped down on the neck permanently and reset its rocket thrusters towards the bottom of the sea. #2's missiles went off, blasting in the direction of the ocean's floor. Both whales were consumed by the hellish blowback and were instantly vaporized.

CELEBRATION

Sasha couldn't stop hugging her dad. They had won the fight. Both whales had decommissioned the other. Green World couldn't finish their plan. World Domination was put on hold. Agent Stones gave each of them a high five. It was the first time Mack saw the stern-faced man smile for real.

"Come on, guys. Good work. Now let's get out of this dump. Xavier's corpse is starting to reek."

Mack agreed. He was tired of looking at death, so he turned to his daughter. He finally had her back in his life. He asked what had happened to Nora. Sasha hung her head low and sobbed. "Xavier…he killed her."

"I'm so sorry. I know we had our differences, but she was still a good woman."

Agent Stones quietly led them out of the facility and back the way they had entered previously.

Mack said to Sasha, as they stepped towards the woods full of dawn's earliest inklings of light, "I'm going to dedicate my life to making this a better world to live in. You and me, Sasha, are going to take life by the reigns and really live life to the fullest. I love you, Sasha. Things happen to us that really make us take pause and realize how good the things in our lives really are."

Before Mack could say another word, a wild stream of machine gun fire was rained down upon them. Mack took four to the chest, and two to the head. Stones covered Sasha with his body, and they both hit the ground.

FRIENDLY FIRE

CIA operatives surrounded them. Agent Stones snarled and raged in anger at the mistake that was made. Huddles of CIA, armed to the teeth, flooded into Green World's secret cave facility. Shortly after, an ambulance was called to pick up Mack's dead body. After he was carted off into a body bag, Agent Stones drew Sasha aside, and tried to help her through this most tragic moment.

"Your father did so much to save the world. He was so brave. I couldn't have done it without him. You terminated the signal that caused those animals to go berserk. There was a second signal, but we've finally traced it, and eliminated it. All because of you and your father. I see him in you, Sasha. I was told those who shot your father thought we were Green World goons. It was an honest mistake, considering our communications have been down, and—"

Sasha spoke over him. She was angry, pissed off, and brimming with venom. "You said it. It was a mistake, and it was caused by Green World. I want to take them down. They're still out there. I know, because Xavier and my mother talked about how evenly dispersed they are throughout the United States and abroad. I want to join the fight. I want to bleed Green World dry, until the organization is a dead carcass wilting in the sun. I'll turn them into compost."

"You really mean that, don't you?"

"My family is dead, my friends were taken from me a long time ago, all because of Green World. Yes, Agent Stones, I really do mean that."

Agent Stones shook her hand. "Then I'll train you. You and me, we'll both take Green World down. We'll turn them into compost. Okay, let's get you out of here. We have work to do."

EPILOGUE

Two years later, and the world had long since collected the dead corpses and buried them and rebuilt ruined cities. Concerns about Battle Whale were long gone and replaced with the constant looming threat of Green World. The United Nations were unanimous: Green World must be destroyed. The fight was ongoing, and to prove it, Sasha, now eighteen, and well-trained in defense and weapons, and well on her way to becoming a member of the CIA, stood in Agent Stones' steed. They were wearing desert camouflage and were hunkered behind a tall sand dune out in the middle of the Gobi Desert, located in Southern Mongolia.

Agent Stones handed her a pair of long-range binoculars. "You see it down there?"

There was a hatch colored of the same sand as the desert. "Yeah, I see it."

"It's a bunker. Green World is hiding down there. There's a think tank going on down there. The highest ranking officials are talking about how to rebuild their signal that drives animals crazy. Those bombs you laid out earlier will cave-in their bunker. Do you care to pull the trigger?"

"Hell yeah, I do!"

Sasha reached for the detonator, and hit the button without a moment's hesitation. "BOOM BITCH!"

Fifteen explosions sent up giant clods of sand. The sand imploded, causing the shape of the bunker to become clear. Sand filled the recesses.

Agent Stones tossed in two bricks of C-4 and unleashed a new round of explosions. "Plug your ears!"

When the dust from the BOOMS settled, and those in the bunker were clearly dead, Agent Stones' radio receiver went off. It was from the Head of the CIA.

"What's going on?" Sasha asked. "They find us another target to destroy? Bring it on."

Agent Stones face went slack. He turned a sickly shade of pale.

"What is it, Stones? Tell me."

Agent Stones collected himself. "There's been reports of activity on the Pacific Ocean."

"Yeah, of what?"

"We have to pack up, and fast."

"What's going on? Why don't you just tell me?" Sasha grabbed Stones by both arms. "You're killing me here. Spit it out."

"Green World's at it again."

"What else is new? Tell me what's going on."

"Green World has a new secret weapon. It's bigger and more deadly than ever."

"And that weapon is?"

Stones had to take a deep breath before he could force himself to say the words.

"There's hundreds of them. *Battle Belugas*."

Fin